Airplane Charlie

Rising Of The Rarri Dynasty

Marcus McBroom

Disclaimer

This is a work of fiction. Names, characters, businesses, places, events and incidents are either the products of the author's imagination or used in a fictitious manner. Any resemblance to actual persons, living or dead, or actual events is purely coincidental.

In accordance with the U.S. Copyright Act of 1976, uploading, scanning and electronic sharing of any part of this book without the sole permission of the publisher constitute unlawful piracy and theft of the author's intellectual property. Written permission is required if you would like to use any part of this book for other than review purposes, prior written permission must be obtained by contacting the publisher at info@newblogtalk.com. Thank you for your support of the author's rights.

Forward

Marcus McBroom reaches out to the soul and heart of his readers with his first novel. He captivates his audience with his ever changing struggles and victories in the hood and in life. He takes you on a journey of growing up on the south side of Columbus; with the constant run in with the law -all the way to Mexico where he deals with dangerous drug cartel. You are there with him in the war between gangs and the heated love between a man and his woman. His words are raw and the dialect is from the streets -no correction, no curving just straight from the hood.

His first novel is riveting, captivating, and funny sometimes. He has done an excellent job to make his reader feel different emotions; elevated and humble.

~Lyn Moses

Dedication

To my children and family, you are never far away; you are my heart and each beat is for you.

I am grateful for the LORD for giving me the talent to make this happen. I would like to say thanks to all my friends and family that supported me through out this long journey. My kids and wife Le'keisha I love y'all so much. My mother and father who always told me to never give up, and the best mother- in -law in the world this one is for you. My whole SQUAD Down Town Much love. This one is for the streets all over the world, it's niggas right here in Columbus who names hold weight. 706 all the way to the 334 it's nothing you can't do if you put yo mind to it.

LOVE: Airplane Charlie Mr. 706

Table Of Contents

Introduction

Introduction

Nothing in the world is more important than blood, but having a complete blood line could prove to be just as important. Doing FED time will do more for you than plug you in, it can also show you how to form the perfect blood line.

Ox was a full blooded Jamaican with connections to more weed than you could ever imagine. His roommate Jose' was a high ranking Mexican with ties to the Triple C. Cartel and MS13. Over a 6 year period of time they were cell mates and made sure their family got to know each other.

Jose' had a daughter named Jessie. Ox had a son named Amari. Ox's son Amari and Jose's daughter Jessie had an amazing little girl named Queen. Jessie already had one older son name King, together that made a house full of royalty. Jessie named her baby girl after the city knowing she would grow up to be somebody of great importance. They grew up in Queen City -Charlotte, North Carolina on easy street.

Ox and Jose was released from prison 4 ½ weeks apart, with plans of taking over the entire South from Va. all the way to Fla. In a matter of months they had their hands in a little of everything. Keys of cocaine were $25,000 and pounds of weed were at a going rate of $600 a pound

Chapter 1 Shoot That Fuckin' Nigga; Charlie

"Shoot that fuck nigga Charlie" (Boom, Boom, Boom)
Three shots to the chest as Pull smashed off in his 1986
two door Box Chevy.   The ride back to B.T.W.
apartments
    seemed to take forever and the palms of Charlie's hands
    were pouring sweat from the adrenaline.   The crack
head they had just shot was trying to turn state on them
(Pull and Fatty had just killed somebody 3 weeks ago) and
Fatty was still in jail being held on a 2 million dollar bond.

    B.T.W. was the smallest projects in Columbus, Ga., but
it was also the meanest. Columbus was a growing city, and
was located next to one of the biggest army bases in the
U.S.A., which made it the second largest city in Ga.
Charlie and Pull grew up in B.T.W.. Marquies Smith had
gotten the name Pull 1, because he was always trying to get
over on folks.   Marcus Smith, aka Charlie, came from
having a nice shot on the dice (One shot Charlie).   As
young boys they made names for themselves by doing
things that would land them in RYDC. Drugs, guns, stolen
cars, anything that had money involved they had a hand in
it.

They made their big break in the streets when they did 48 months in RYDC for gang related activity for a shooting that happened inside the Peachtree Mall. After being out for a mere 8 months they were neck deep in trouble with the law again facing life sentence if found guilty. 8:00 A.M.; the next morning the phone rang. Marcus father was calling early, *"Son, I don't know what you and Pull done got y'all self into, but the police just kicked my door in looking for y'all about a murder."*

"Murder? I don't know nothing about that shit. I wasn't even with them when they did that shit."

"They stressing that Rarri Gang shit, I done told y'all about that fuckin' shit," he said angrily.

"Fasho pop, but I know I was in the projects with Kee when that shit happen," Marcus replied.

"You a grown man now, so I ain't gon' tell you what to do, but you need to lay low. If you can make it to this weekend I'll take you to North Carolina," pops said with concern.

"Bet dad"

"Stay out the way man, cause if they get you before we come up with money for a lawyer it's going to be over for you son," pops said to Marcus hoping he was listening.

"Already know it dad."

Marcus' mother and three sisters lived in Charlotte. Really his whole family mother side and father lived up there. Like Columbus, Charlie knew Charlotte like the back of his hand. So once he got up there his run would last much longer. From selling dope Charlie had only saved up $4,300, he already knew he was gone rob a few niggas to get the rest of the lawyer money. Three days later on a Sunday Charlie's father paid a friend of his to take him up the road. A five hour ride in the trunk of the car, was the worst ride ever. But a nigga will do anything to keep his freedom. It was what it was

Chapter 2 Gangster Or Crip

In Columbus; you are one or two things, Gangsta or Crip. Other than that; most people repped their hoods, Uptown, South Side, East Side, E-Dud, West Side, and Downtown. B.T.W. was Downtown which would be the West Side of town. Back in the day E-Canty projects started saying they was the West Side also. All the young boys Downtown started repping "Rarri Gang", (a ruthless gang from Downtown) to let it be known which projects went the hardest. In B.T.W. Rarri was a noun; it could be used as a person, place or thing. It was like Master P saying "BOUT IT, BOUT IT" in the 90's. It didn't mean shit at first but when it blew, that bitch blew.

One Friday after school Jason, Trick, Pull, Money and Charlie were walking through the mall; window shopping and checking out the girls. The projects was rolling and all week they had been spending money; The Teen Jam was tomorrow. While inside Foot Locker, Charlie met La'Kee his soon to be baby momma. While exchanging numbers four boys from the East Side walked into the store.

The tall one bumped Charlie, "*Move Nigga!*"

Charlie was six days away from being 14 years old and Pull was already 14. Buddy had to be about 20. The youngest of the four "East Siders" was about 18.

"*Pussy ass Nigga, who you talking to, bump me like that again I know somethin'*", Charlie said looking the guy in the eye.

"*Lil' bitch ass nigga you know what fuck you talking bout,*" he said with one hand up in Charlie's face and the other inside his sagging jean pants.

Without thinking Charlie slapped the shit out of buddy, dropping him to the floor. His homeboy quickly rushed Charlie, sending him to the floor. (Boom, Boom, Boom) Charlie quickly made it to his feet and saw Money standing there, gun in hand. Charlie glanced to his left and notice one of the dudes had been shot trying to run out the store. When he saw it was Buddy who had started it all, Charlie ran behind him pulling his 32 revolver from his waist band.

Boom! Boom! Boom! Boom! Boom! Boom! Shooting all six bullets out the gun he had hit him in the leg. You could hear Pull yelling, "*Rarri Gang Bitch*!"

When the smoke cleared and everything was all said and done, they were all put in jail. They were charged with everything under the sun- 34 aggravated assaults to four gun charges and all kinds of gang shit.

After reviewing the mall surveillance tape the judge said he wish he could hold them all till they were 21 years old.

During the time it seem like every kid from Columbus was repping Rarri. Half of them didn't know Charlie but they treated him like he was Hoover.

Charlie was Bossed up like a motherfucker, all those lil' niggas did what he said. If he said ride, they were going to tear that bitch up.

Charlie was move to seven different camps in 48 months. All were C-Town, and the camp was deep. He had that motherfucker on smash.

You were either, "Squad Life Or No Life".

Queen was a super bad bitch to be 18. Dark brown skin complexion, 5'9 and right at 135 pounds. She had nice size breast with a waist "34-24-36" , nice cola shape. In the south there was nothing better than a chick with a fat ass. Both of their dreads were about the same size and hung a little pass the shoulders. Her dreads stood out with the three different colors she had. Everyday Queen would walk laps around the apartment where Charlie's mom lived. Every time they saw each other they would lock eyes and smile. Charlie notice the gold in her mouth. Knowing she smoked weed was a big plus because Charlie hadn't smoke shit since he had been away.

"*Say shawty, where can I get some green at*?", Charlie called out to Queen.

"*Shawty? You can't be from around here. My name is Queen*", she said proudly.

"*I'm sorry Ms Lady. I'm just trying to smoke one*", he said in a soft deep voice.

"You can smoke this one with me, right here".

"*I been seeing you working out and shit everyday now. You*

fine as a mutherfucer too, if I must say", Charlie said flashing his stunning smile.

"I can't be too fine if it took you three days to notice me", she snapped back with her hands on her hips.

Queen couldn't wait to get home and call her home girl.

"Guess what bitch, I got his number now...."

"Okay call me when he leave"

She laid across her bed thinking. Dam a bitch had to do a fake workout plan everyday to get a nigga (laughing). We got the same gold teeth and all. Marcus and Queen he said that shit sound good together. I can't let this nigga ever leave Charlotte.

Chapter 3 Guns Blazin' On Independent Blvd

It had been a few days since Charlie talked to anyone back home. He had not spoken to Pull either. After going without speaking to his boy for a week and a half Pull called to holla at his boy.

"What it do, baby boi?"

"Shit bra', just trying to lay low for a hot min", he said in a lazy voice.

"Where you at bra NC?".

(laughing) "*Hell yeah. How you know?*" Charlie was curious to know how Pull knew his whereabouts because he was careful not to leave any clues around. At least he thought he did.

"*Come on bra' you know I know what time it is. (laughing) Yo girl bout to have a lil' nigga in a couple of days?*"

"Hell yeah. I know she hot too cause I ain't called her or nothin'."

"I was just getting me a lil' check run in bra. Much love. I'll fuck with you later", said Pull.

"Fasho, much love bra".

As Charlie was getting off the phone with Pull the doorbell rung.

It was Queen, *"You want to smoke?"*

Queen had a 530i BMW, baby powder blue with gray interior parked outside. They rode around the entire city blowing. Queen made a few stops. For some reson she kept going in the trunk of the car. Charlie didn't ask any questions the entire time, but he had a 357 automatic on him in case anything even look crazy; it was going down. He was going to be running from a body in both places if he had to shoot someone. Shawty was a cool lil' chick. Charlie could tell she had something going on because she made too many dam stops. The lil' bitch pussy was so good he really wasn't too concern about that other shit.

She was slick and had Charlie fucked up on the low.

Coming down Independent Blvd smoking a blunt of Dro, Charlie notice a grey Mazda 626 in the rear view mirror, he didn't tink too much of it at first. The past days they were just kicking, no stops at all, now today, they made one stop on North Tron St and this was the same car tailing them for an hour. Charlie cut the radio down on Queen to make sure he wasn't tripping. When they made the next left you could see two niggas in the with dreads.

"Bae, what the fuck you keep going in that trunk for?", he said with irritation in his voice.

"Nothin' bae", she replied with a teasing and very sexy voice.

Ordinarily her voice would make Charlie knees weak, but right now some niggas were walking up on them and he immediately became focus on his surroundings. Charlie pulled out his 357.

"Bitch! Why are these niggas following us if it's nothing?"

"*Where?*" She almost lost control of the car looking in the rear view mirror.

"*Man hoe; you better get right before you kill us in here*".

"*You don't have to talk to me like that Marcus*" (all the sexiness went out of her voice and the itch sounded like a gangster chic down for whatever).

"*Listen bitch; I am talking to you like that bitch because I'm on the run for murder and you got me out here fumbling. What's in the fucking trunk?*"

"*Cake Marcus cake. I don't know how much or nothing'. I just drop it off and pick up the money for my dad. You happy now I told you?*" she said sounding like a victim -simple girl.

"*Hoe let me out this car. I ain't bout to get killed fucking with yo ass. Let me out at this gas station up here*".

"*Really Marcus. You on the run for murder?*"

"*Bitch, if you don't let me out this fucking car I'm gon'*

shoot the shit out yo' dumb ass".

Once they pulled in the gas station; still fussing, they notice the Mazda was still on their tail.

"Man, please tell me you got a strap in this car and it's not in the trunk".

"Yeah, it's one inside the glove box. Why?"

The Mazda pulled up on Charlie's side of the car and a black Grand AM pulled behind them. Queen had a baby glock 40. Cal in the glove box. As Charlie moved toward exiting the car the driver of the Mazda was getting out too. The barrow of the 9mm riffle he had was so long it took him one second too many to get out the car. Boom!

When Charlie saw the gun he shot homes point blank range in the face with the 357. The passenger of the Mazda took off running when he heard that loud ass gun shot. Charlie let about six more shots go towards the one trying to out run the glock 40, until he heard Bang, Bang, Bang, Bang,

Bang, Bang, Bang, Bang, Bang, Bang, Bang!

Looking back to see a nigga hanging out the back window of the Grand AM gunning. Putting one of the pistols on his hip to help Queen all the bullets was hitting her side of the car. You could tell she was hit. Charlie used his left hand to pull Queen across the seat. Homes was still shooting.

He tossed her inside the Mazda, "BAE GET THE MONEY."

Charlie reach over the seat of the BMW popping the trunk, it was two bags inside the trunk, a Jordan gym bag and a purse. You could see all the money inside the purse. Trying to get the fuck away from the crime scene, Queen had been shot twice in the leg and side. Using her own cell phone to call her brother King.

"Hey folk yo sister just got shot".

"What? She ok, who the fuck is this?"

"Hell nah, she not ok, she been hit twice".

"We on our way to the hospital" he said yelling at some family members who were listening closely in the background to him on the phone. Queen been shot".

Charlie rolled his eyes. He never said where he was or what hospital. Niggas just thinking what they want. They watch too much dam TV.

"Look I'm not going to jail, we like three minutes away from y'all crib, I'm bout to bring her over there".

King and his mother and father was outside when Charlie pulled up with Queen in the car. Mrs. Jessie, her mother was freaking out, so was King. That let Charlie know it wasn't know way possible the family knew she was making the runs for her dad. After getting Queen in the truck with her mother, Charlie handed Amari the Jordan bag that had the work in it. There was no way in hell Charlie was giving up the purse with the money in it. When Charlie made it to his momma house from ducking the Mazda off and counted that money it was 37 bands. All he could say was "JACK POT"!!!!!

Chapter 4 Get Out Of The House Now Son; They Coming

For three days Charlie wouldn't answer Queen's phone calls. He wasn't responding to her text messages either. The big shoot out at the gas station was all over the **NEWS**. It was to the point Charlie cut his hair to change up his look. The police said they found over 75 shell cases, 52 of them went in to the side of Queen's BMW. The phone rung, it was Le'Kee. It was about that time to drop the baby, that's the only reason he answered her call.

"Dam stranger", she said in a painful voice.

"What it do baby girl".

"So, you wasn't gon' tell me you was up there staying with yo mamma?"

"How the baby doing y'all good?".

"Lame ass nigga. You don't care how me and my baby doing. You been gone almost a month now".

"Man hoe, I'm not trying to hear all that shit. I got bigger problems".

"That's why they got Pull last night and yo fuckin' ass next BITCH"

CLICK. She hung up the phone in Charlie's ears. Charlie just knew that hoe was flexing, he called Pull over and over getting no answer. So he call Amanda, Pull's sister and she gave him the run down on what happened. His big cuz explained how they got Pull out the Motel room; somebody set him up. As Charlie was on the phone talking to Amanda, his mother beeped in on the other line.

"What's up Ma?"

"GET OUT THE HOUSE NOW, SON THEY COMING!"

Charlie drop the phone when he heard his mother say those words. Looking out the upstairs window you could see unmarked cars pulling up in front of the house.

Charlie ran to his baby sister Nala's room and jumped clean out the second floor window. The 6 feet tall pool in the back yard saved him from the police seeing him as they came rushing around the house. Every bit of 45 officers ran in the house once they kick the back door in. Lord knows what the front looked like. Charlie knew it was now or never, he peeked to see if anyone was in clear sight and hit the gate.

Charlie didn't stop or look back, he kept running all through people yards until he made it to the park where he had the Mazda 626 parked. The best thing Charlie did was cut his hair. The police was everywhere. They had the entire apartment complex fucked up and Charlie just knew it was over for him. The SWAT TEAM had just got there and a female officer was standing at the top of the road. The female officer kept saying "Clear the street it's a murder suspect in the complex." She let Charlie slip right pass her. They got the address from written letters he had wrote to Le'Kee while he was in RYDC. She had sent letters to his mothers' address also so they knew the address. There was no if ands or buts about it who sent the police. Charlie made his mind up he was going back home. But he had to make one stop before he dip, that was to see Queen in the hospital.

Queen had been in the hospital four days now. She sent text messages saying she was in room 215; if he wanted to see her. From losing so much blood the doctor wouldn't let her leave the hospital. Walking up to the room door Charlie could hear the conversation Queen and her brother was having.

"Sis I couldn't get in the house to get them clothes for you. The cops had that shit fucked up. They was showing pictures of yo boyfriend saying he killed somebody in Georgia".

"Dam, I wondering if they got him or not".

"What the hell you doing around him if you knew all that? That fool got niggas trying to kill him and shit. Now you in here fighting for your life".

"King shut the fuck up, you don't know what you're talking bout. If it wasn't for Marcus being on point my life would be over. He the reason I'm still alive right now".

Mrs. Jessie told them both that was enough, she didn't want to hear any more about it. Everybody needed to be thankful that Queen and Marcus was alive, because it's one man who didn't make it home from that store, and they were dam lucky. Listening to them talk Charlie never saw the two detectives sitting directly across from the room. Queens face widen with a smile , from ear to ear when he walked into the room. Mrs. Jessie jumped up and hugged Charlie so tight "Thank you so much, she told me everything "

"Bae you cut your hair?"

"You must not be feeling the new look".

"I love everything about you Marcus. You could cut your head off I'll still want you", she said laughing.

Charlie couldn't do nothing but smile. He could feel Mrs. Jessie hug him again from behind saying "THANK YOU LORD". King had a look on his face like he wanted to say something but he looked lost for words.

Standing there with his fist balled up, Charlie had to ask him what was on his mind.

"My nigga, you look like you got something you want to say".

"Nigga you almost got my sister killed".

"One; you don't have a ounce of black in you so choose your choice of words more carefully. And two; she is thereason I almost got killed, you need to get yo facts straight. Fuck you talking bout nigga".

"You are a real pussy, I'll kick yo motherfuckin' ".

Mrs. Jessie had just let Charlie go, King didn't even get a chance to finish his statement. He dam near swallowed all four elbows Charlie hit him with. King was laying in the bed next to Queen after Charlie hit him.

The licks was so loud and hard all kinds of people burst into the room. King had blood all over his clothes. The detectives locked eyes with Charlie and grab him off the rip, slamming him to the ground.

Queen yelled "All that shit not called for."

The doctor was stressing as he said, "GET HIM OUT OF HERE".

Charlie couldn't believe he just let that fuckin' nigga trick him off the streets like that when he had just escaped the police not even 20 minutes ago.

After Marcus was finger printed and records scan; murder and all kind of charges popped up ASAP. Looking at the mug shot of him with hair they question him about the gas station shooting. Charlie asked for a lawyer, the Mecklenburg County police got in touch with Muscogee County and within 14 hours they were there to pick him up.

Chapter 5 "Pussy Ass Nigga"

Ox and Jose both came in town to get a better understanding to what the fuck happen to their granddaughter. Amari knew he was in some deep shit when he saw Jose come in the front door behind his father. It was normal for the family to see Ox, he didn't live too far away, in Rock Hill S.C.. On top of that, Ox made sure all the business got handle for Jose. Jose was living in Dallas TX to be closer to the connect and to stay off the scene. Queen couldn't walk, so soon as Jose came in the house he went straight for his granddaughter, helping her down the stairs into the living room. Jose pace the floor, back and forth after seeing the two gunshot wounds that Queen had suffered. Jose called everybody in the living room for a house meeting.

"Our family is strong, due to the fact we made it through a lot of shit. There are rules we set from day one and goals that are to be accomplished. So whatever jack ass felt it was ok for my only granddaughter to be trafficking drugs can't cherish and must not value his life".

"Jose with all due respect it wasn't us, the young boy she was with had something to do with the shooting".

"Amari I'm not going to let you bad mouth Marcus like this. Father Marcus is the only reason Queen is still here with us now. That young man was in the blind and didn't have to help our child get out that car. He could have left her there to die. And as long as I got breath in my body I'm going to help him. He wouldn't even be in jail if it wasn't for all this nonsense".

"What matters right now is that she is ok. And Amari to be honest with you the only reason you are still alive is because of the love I have for your father. So please shut the fuck up. Any other careless mistake will end with your life do I make myself clear?"

"I, understand".

Queen never told her grandfather the real run down on what her father really was doing cause she knew they would have killed him. But she did let it be known that Marcus saved her life and all the money she had saved up she was about to put it on a lawyer for him.

This was Charlie's first time going to the county, stressing, popping Xpills, and smoking weed Charlie lost weight in 10 months.

After being processed in the jail they sent Charlie upstairs to the 5th floor to dorm 519. He was put in a dorm filled with all the murderers, armed robbers, and young black boys with big charges. They didn't even mix white boys and black boys in the same dorms. Lil Pee Wee from the East Side was the first person Charlie saw walking in the dorm.

"What's up bra?"

"Pull is up there in room 16 bra."

Pee Wee had killed a white man about a year ago on the South Side over some crack. Niggas started coming out there rooms when they saw Charlie. Pull couldn't believe it when Charlie walked in his room.

"What's up bra? I just was telling bra last night when I saw you on the News they need to bring you in here. What them folks talking bout you killed somebody in N.C. bra?"

"Hell yeah that shit was crazy, you good doe"

"I'm good bra, we just in here kicking it".

"What the fuck wrong with yo' eye Rarri?"

"That fuckin' nigga J-Byrd son in here and we got the hitting the other night bout you shooting his daddy. He is slick, got the best of me but, it ain't no big deal".

Already hot about Pull's eye J-Byrd sent one of his flunky in the room, *"Say Charlie Byrd what are you in the pit for folk?"*.

"What the fuck is the pit Pull?"

"Man these niggas tripping. I think the nigga want to fight bra".

Off the rip Charlie took his shirt off and flew out the door looking for the pit. Everybody was gather down stairs. An old School cat from B.T.W. yelled,

"Oh I'm telling y'all dis right now ain't nobody bout to jump on my lil homie."

That was all Charlie needed to hear somebody was going to ride with him. Charlie locked eyes with J-Byrd and they squared up. The two punches J-Byrd threw Charlie he blocked them. J-Byrd fucked up when he got frustrated and tried to rush Charlie; Charlie side stepped him to the left and caught him in the eye with a right hook. That wasn't the lick that counted.

The left elbow sent J-Byrd into the cell door, busting his noise off the rip. When Charlie saw J-Byrd was down and he was trying to block his face, Charlie drop down to one knee and punched J-Byrd in the stomach. Coming back up with an elbow to the chin. As J-Byrd fell to his knees Charlie kneed his butt 15 times in the face. With every lick you could hear Charlie saying *"PUSSY ASS NIGGA."*

His old school homie boy had to grab Charlie and tell him *"It's over lil bra."*

In so much rage, Charlie couldn't even hear J-Byrd saying *"you got it folk"* over and over.

Turning around to walk back up the stairs Charlie saw the nigga who came and told him J-Byrd wanted him standing at the bottom of the steps. Charlie grabbed him by the shirt and elbow his ass clean out.

"Yeah fuck nigga the messenger get it to."

Buddy fell flat out on his face. You could see two of his teeth laying on the floor beside him in the puddle of blood.

Pee Wee was standing on the table talking shit. "I knew that nigga couldn't do nothin' with Charlie, Me and bra was just down the road together in Eastman GA., they was calling bra Airplane the way he was taking flight on them young niggas."

Charlie was still mad as hell, he knew the situation he was in and this might be where he had to spend the rest of his life, because snitching was out the question. Watching what room J-Byrd went in, Charlie went right behind him closing the door as he walked in the cell.

"I'm done folk you got it".

"Pussy ass nigga, now I got it huh? Yo fuck ass didn't let my brother have it".

"He shot my daddy folk".

"I'm the one who shot that police ass nigga, now what".

"You got it folk".

"Nigga I ain't no folk, this shit Rarri".

J-Byrd saw where things were headed, Charlie had already lock them in the room. Byrd was two times Charlie size.

Only thing he could think to do was rush Charlie up against the door. Before Charlie back hit the cell door, he hit J-Byrd in the mouth about 8 times, back to back. Grabbing J- Byrd by the neck slamming his head into the concrete wall, blood was everywhere. J-Byrd had fell in the bed knocked out cold Charlie was still punching him in the face when Pull got to the door and popped in the room to break it up.

"Chill bra you gon' kill that fool bra, we already got enough shit going on".

"Fuck this nigga, let me kill'em".

"On some real Rarri shit bra. Let that shit go. Fuck that nigga, it ain't worth it, straight up bra".

Charlie let him go but he swore on every dead person in his family, that if any one of these other niggas in here tried him he was going to be charged with 2 bodies in this bitch.

Chapter 6 Bond For This "Catch A Body" Case

The murder case was getting the best of Charlie especially knowing he didn't have anything to do with it. During the time of the murder he was nowhere near the vicinity when the shit happened. The unfortunate part; if one nigga goes down we all go down.

They didn't have to worry too much about food and shit like that with the money Charlie took from Amari and his mother was sending him 300$ a month. Mom got him two good lawyers Eddy Johnson and Bob Cater. A small amount of money coming in from others was a blessing too, and it all added up at the end of the day.

The past 5 months passed by fast as hell. Le'Kee had just had her son and named him Ja'Marcus Smith. Queen would write Charlie once a week (that nigga wouldn't even read the letters better yet respond to them). Out of the blue one Saturday morning the guard called "*Charlie Marcus Smith Viso.*" Pull had a visitation at the same time. Only person who came to see Charlie was his father and Le'Kee from time to time, and they would beef real bad (he could not blame her ass for those moments).

Queen was sitting in the second Chair waiting on me next to Pull sister Shun. That mufucker know she sexy. Even her mother was there with her, both of them had on the same shirt with my picture on it that said, "FREE MY CHARLIE RARRI).

"Hey son, how you been doing? And why you don't be calling us boy?".

"I'm good ma, for real I don't be calling nobody".

"Boy I'm glad Queen got to see you cause she been driving me crazy. Has Mr. Cater come by to see you yet? He has good things to say every time I talk to him".

"Yea I just talked to him last week, I ain't know y'all been checking on me like that".

"You know I love you, I spent 25,000$ on yo ass I got to love you. Well I'm not gon take all of your time up I just wanted to see your face and tell you I love you. Start calling; we got minutes on all the phones".

"I will love you to Mrs. Jessie".

Mrs. Jessie got up waved and walked off. Queen was sitting there with a mad look on her face but you could tell she was excited to see Charlie.

Pull peeked in the booth to see her face.

"That must be Queen Rarri." Charlie shook his head yeah. "Damm that mufucker fine bra."

"Long time no see or hear from Mr. Charlie".

"Already know it, how you been doing doe".

"Going crazy worried about you, have you been getting the money I been sending you every month bae".

"Yea I been getting it, and thank you too".

"Marcus I know you hate me for being the reason you are in here or however you feel. But I promise you I'm doing everything in my power to get you out of here. I love you I'm so sorry this happen like this. Please just talk to me, call me, write me back, let me help make this hard time a lil easier for you, that's all I'm asking. I swear to GOD I'll never keep anything from you again. You just don't know how much you mean to me Marcus".

"Stop crying man, I'm fucking with you. You better understand loyalty mean everything to me".

"I understand Marcus, I love you and miss you so fucking much. All I do is think about you".

"I love you to bae".

"When I leave from here I'm gon' take Lil Marc this stuff me and ma got for him if that's okay with you. It's a bunch of shit too bae".

"Go head bae that's cool".

The visit didn't last but 30 minutes but she came back that Sunday and let Charlie know as long as he was fucking with her she would come see him twice a month. Kee was hot cause she wanted to be back with Charlie. Queen had his heart, plus shawty was one of a kind a nigga and he would be a fool to let her go.

Charlie and Pull set up in the room and read all the letters she had written the entire time he been locked up. Queen told him everything about herself, including the fact , her grandfathers were kingpins. She did not leave out how her father didn't like him too much; but he respect what she had going on. For some reason the doctor told her she couldn't have kids, but the most important part of it all was that when this shit was all said and done her grand dad was going to put him on. Queen sent him over 40 pictures of herself that Charlie had never seen. She even told him Mr. Cater had been working to get Charlie a bond on the murder case. Queen was stressing; it didn't matter how much it cost she wanted him to get out the same day.

Chapter 7 What This Bitch Got Me Into Now

After being locked up 8 months one morning out of no where the guard came in the dorm and got Charlie and took him down stairs. Charlie didn't know where they were going, he just followed suit. They ended up in the front of the jail adjacent to the recorders court. Mr. Johnson was standing there waiting on him to walk up.

"How are you Mr. Smith? We are attempting to get you a bond. Once we get inside of the court room don't say a word, let me do all the talking okay? I'll take that as a yes", he said laughing.

The D.A. made his case that I might run due to the fact that I was apprehended in N.C.. He also stated, I had too many high rank charges, concluding that I was a threat to society. Mr. Johnson read some code Texas V.S the United States and before you knew it the judge was giving Charlie a bond on everything 250,000 for murder, 20,000 on the aggravated assault, 10,000 on the gun charge, and 50,000for tampering with evidence. Sending Charlie back.

"Well Marcus, I've done my part now it's your family's turn to get you out. I'll get in touch with your mother and let her know how much the bonds are set for".

"Thanks Mr. Johnson".

"You are welcome son".

Charlie was in a rush to get back upstairs to call Queen and tell her how much the bond was to get him out, 330,000$ it would take every bit of 35,000$ cash or a house worth that much to get him out. Talking to Charlie, Queen didn't sound like she had a worry in the world about coming up with the money. Only thing she said was give her till the weekend and she would be in Columbus to come get him.

Thirty-five bands was a lot of money to come up with. Pull had more faith in Queen then Charlie did. That night before they went to sleep Charlie told Pull if he got out- no matter what it took he was going to get Fatty a lawyer, he couldn't let his cousin be the only one to go in the court room without representation.

The very next morning about 10:15 the guard came in the dorm yelling *"Marcus Smith roll it up you made bond"* just like that it was over with.

Charlie couldn't believe shawty came up with the money that fast. It took every bit of an hour to do all the paper work and to get processed out of the jail. Queen was the first person Charlie saw when he walked out the doors holding Lil Marc. Mrs. Jessie was there with them too.

Queen couldn't stop hugging and kissing on Charlie *"I told you I was going to do whatever it took to get you back on these streets. My granddaddy Jose gave me the money to get you out bae he wants to talk to you."*

She just couldn't stop talking. He knew Mrs. Jessie played a major part in getting him out as well. King was sitting outside in the car waiting on me. He gave Charlie some dap and a hug.

"Dam bra you done got big as hell. I know you happy to be out that hell hole".

"Hell yea boy that county jail biting. I ain't lying".

"Sorry about what happen between us hope we can overlook the bullshit".

"We fam' bra, what happen in the past stay in the past, we got to move on. You feel me".

Lil Marc couldn't stop smiling from the time he laid eyes on his daddy.

After Charlie and Queen came from seeing his father, she told him her grandfather Ox and her dad was in town and they wanted to see him. They all met up at Ryan's off of Manchester Expressway.

Queen parked next to her grandfather's money green BMW 745. *"Let me talk to Marcus for a second Queen and he will be inside shortly sweetheart."* Charlie got in the car behind Amari.

"My grandbaby is madly in love with you son, so don't take it for granted. Jose sent me here to explain to you how you are going to work this 40 grand tab off. My son Amari here is the boss of this situation, what he says goes, no questions asked.

"My people will be here in less than 10 hours to bring you 5 kilos of cocaine 27,000$ each. Ten good runs we should be in the clear. Here take this cell phone and guard it with your life. Because the first time you don't answer it I promise you I will kill you, not just you but your family as well.

My granddaughter doesn't need to have any recollection of what we have going on what so ever. My number is programmed in the phone under Lord cause right now that is who I am to you GOD. Do we have a understanding son?".

"Yeah, real clear".

"Okay, now get out my car".

Walking in the restaurant all Charlie kept saying to himself was *"what this bitch got me into now."* He wasn't out two good hours and he was already into deep, 135,000$.

Chapter 8 Gangster Love

The whole B.T.W. was happy to see Charlie, the hood thought he was gone- just another lost soldier -lost to the system. The whole city knew I was out; thanks to the news for reporting about how I made that high ass bond.

Nurge was one of the homies from the hood making a lil' noise with the work on the street. He informed Charlie about the cocaine drought in the city. Niggas was riding all the way to Atlanta to get work. The weed game was just as fucked up too. Making a normal round through the projects with Queen like any nigga would do fresh out, Charlie notice that it wasn't hardly no crack in the hood. Crack heads were everywhere, but it wasn't an ounce of dope downtown.

Charlie was a young nigga the OG's loved for never being follower. When he got out of juvenile Bubba set him down and explained to him the game on how to get some real money. Showed him how to cook dope. On a bad day Charlie could take 28 grams of soft to about 39, but on a good one he could get the dope up in the low 40's.

Columbus was a gold mine for a nigga with a lot of work because an ounce of hard only weighed 24 grams. You couldn't do much, but win if you knew how to cook. Charlie went back to the hotel room and sent Queen to Walmart to get him some Pyrex pots. When she got back Charlie didn't waste any time he cooked 2 keys up and turn them into 117 ounces. With three keys, a quarter brick, and 1,000 piece, Charlie was about to fuck the streets up.

With the three keys of powder Charlie had left, he pulled one of Rarri Boys to the side and told them he had a plug and his people could do the zips of soft for 900$ each. Charlie knew how high the dope was out there and it was jug on the whole city selling zips for 11 and 1,200$. He would have downtown to himself and the chance to go ham in the city. What made the squad go even harder was Charlie told them if they showed him they could move the dope quickly, he would be able to flood them with the work.

King felt Charlotte was getting old and wanted to stay in Columbus. That made things even better. King was a Mexican all he had to do was bring the soft to Charlie every time somebody wanted something and he made 75$ off each ounce.

Everybody made a lil somethin'. Nurge was buying 6 zips a day, not including the other zips he would cap off of. The third day with the work was the first of the month and we was getting off like the Dream Team in '96. That day alone we did 13 zips and Charlie got off 15 zips of crack alone.

For the past two days Queen had been tripping.

"What's wrong bae? You look upset".

"I'm ok".

"No you not bae, talk to me, man what's up love bug?".

"I don' everything in my power to get you out of jail. And I feel like you saying fuck me. All you been doing since you been out is selling dope. Where my fucking time at? That's what's wrong with me".

"Yo folks want that fucken bond money back, what am I suppose to be doing?"

"Fuck them. Hell, you can spend some fucking time with me. All I do is sit in this dam room. I want to go home".

"Well take yo mufucken' ass home then. You the reason all this shit going on anyway".

"Nigga I didn't tell yo ass to kill no dam body. You had all that shit going on before I met you. But never forget I'm

the only reason you back out here", she said with her hands on her hips and her head swinging from side to side.

"Bitch you the reason I owe yo folks 100 racks, you don't ever forget that", he said with anger and passion building up inside him.

"I'm going home Marcus".

"Bye!"

Queen packed all her stuff and left without saying another word. She took the rental car she had got for Charlie to get around and left her Lexus GS 430 with him.

King stayed; he had fell in love with Columbus and he said he wasn't never leaving.

It took 15 days to get off the 5 kilos. Charlie made 71 bands profit, putting 31 up and adding 40 on top of the 135 and heading back to charlotte to meet up with Ox. Charlie called Ox on the way.

"Please tell me it's nothing wrong with my money".

"Oh! Money good Rarri. I was just calling to tell you that I put them 40 in there for you. I'm not big on owing people. These next few runs I just want to build a relationship with you and show you I am a standup guy".

"Say no more son, I'll let Jose know".

To try and fix things with Queen he went downtown charlotte and rented a room at the Hyatt Hotel on South Caldwell Street and got a sweet on the 13th floor for 825$ a night. Charlie put rose petals all over the room. Candles all around the tub, order white wine and lobster tails for them to eat. It took a lot of begging to get Queen to meet him at the hotel, but she came because she loved Charlie.

"Listen Queen, words can't explain how I feel about you. I love you so much and I'm man enough to say I was wrong for talking to you in that tone of voice the other day".

"You are to disrespectful Marcus and I just can't deal with a nigga talking to me like this".

"Put yourself in my place, when you ask me for a second chance I gave it to you, now you owe me one".

"I don't owe you shit. I got you out, paid for your lawyer and turn you on to my people. And you can't even watch your fucken mouth".

"You are so right, you don't owe me shit I owe you everything. So I'm asking you for a second chance. I want to be a part of your life. And I promise you from this day forward I will treat you like the Queen you are".

"Boy I love yo ugly ass so much it's sad".

After having the long conversation down stairs in the lobby of the hotel Charlie took Queen to the room. When she saw how he decorated the room for her, she leaped in his arms kissing him with a big Kool Aid smile on her face.

Charlie held Queen in his arms closing the door behind him. Walking her to the bed laying Queen on her back. Taking her clothes off piece by piece. She just laid there going with the flow.

After undressing her, Charlie began to kiss her on her neck, down to her chess, then her stomach, till he got to the middle of her legs were he was licking on her thighs. Queen didn't see Charlie get the ice he had on the floor by the bed. Her eyes was close anyway she was in heaven at the moment.

Opening her pussy lips up as she held her own legs. Sliding the ice cube inside of her pussy with his tongue, Charlie felt Queen's body jump and tense up.

Rubbing the ice slowly across her click as he licked her spur tongue. "Baby I can't take it!" Rubbing his head as Charlie sucked on her pussy until the ice was gone. You could see cum running down the crack of her ass. Queen's body was trembling, she couldn't control it. Going inside of her Queen wrapped her arms around Charlie kissing him, you could see her cum all in his facial hair.

They made love all night until the sun came up. Laying there sleep Charlie rubbed her hair smoking a cigarette thinking *"I'm going to marry this bitch."*

Chapter 9 Rarri Gang Bigger Than Ever

Amari had called and told Charlie to meet him at his house. Queen went in the house to show her mother what Charlie had gave her.

In the meantime; Amari and Charlie stood on the front porch and talked. The look on Amari's face told Charlie that he had some bullshit on his mind.

"Marcus what do your friends call you".

"Airplane Charlie".

"LOL ok Airplane, if you need some more work you don't have to go behind my back and call my father, talk to me and we will work something out".

"I don't know what the fuck you talking bout, I didn't ask him for shit I just told him I had the 40 bands that I owed him".

"Well I'm just letting you know for future references. I got 8 keys and 50 pounds for you, do you think you can handle it or not".

"Hell yeah, I can handle anything you give me even a hit".

"241 is the ticket".

They shook hands and went into the house to eat dinner.

The next morning Charlie, King and Nurge headed back to Columbus. Charlie and Queen had got a good understanding that in a few weeks she could come to Columbus and find them a house. But first he had to get Fatty a lawyer, before his court date popped up.

Charlie cooked up 5 of the 8 keys and turned it into 9 bricks. They broke the weed all the way down 25 pounds in QP's and the other 25 down to Oz's. 50$ a zip. Charlie knew them bitches was going to fly.

King was enjoying being in Columbus fucking hoes and getting his own money. Amari never gave him a chance when she found out that it wasn't his son.

Two weeks with the weed King was turned up bad. King was getting off the weed better then Charlie. In no time they was moving 5 keys a week and 100 pounds of mid.

King had a Mego who was buying 50 pounds every 6 or 7 days. Charlie had paid a lawyer name Carl Williams 18,000$ to take Fatty's case.

Jose took Queen to the All Star Weekend, he asked about King. She told him, King and Charlie was two peas in a pot. He loved the sound of that.

"Queen; Airplane is the grandson I always wanted. The sky is the limit for him."

The Rarri Gang was bigger than ever. Charlie was only 19 moving like a real MOB Boss. Throughout the city, Charlie was fucking with all the young niggas that was rocking with him when he was in RYDC. The fact that they all wanted some money made shit even better. He gave every last one of them packages, letting them see it was Squad Life or No Life for real. Everybody had enough work. It was imperative they didn't fuck up, but if they did, there was an allowance as long as they had most of the money, Charlie would let them work it off on the next one.

Riding through the city, Charlie was throwing up how big R's stressing SQUAD making him feel like a young DON in the C-Town. Once the case was no longer an issue hanging over his head

Charlie would try and link up all these lil niggas all over Georgia. But facing a life sentence in prison for a body, Charlie needed to run up a check, in case he had to go on the run. Doing 20 or 30 years was not an option for Charlie.

King was rocking strong with a Crip nigga from Uptown name lil Sosa. Sosa was from Wilson Projects. Charlie couldn't do anything but fuck with the lil nigga every week, he was moving a 9 of hard and 5 pounds of mid.

Today had been a great day for the team and Nurge, Sosa and King had tricked Charlie into going out for the first time. The Sky Box was the number one club on a Friday night in the city. The line outside was unbelievable with hoes from everywhere. It cost 40 dollars to jump the line. Walking in the club a sexy ass redbone bitch was telling her friend, "Gurl that's that nigga Airplane Charlie from downtown. Right there bitch."

Charlie looked back and smiled like hell- showing all the gold in his mouth.

When they got inside the club D.J. Stone was on the ones and two's, he spotted Charlie and turn the music down and yelled on the mic, *"Shout out to all the real niggas in this bitch, I see a G4 in this bitch, the owner of the Airline, the youngest, realest nigga in the fucking city my nigga, the Rarri Gang Mob Boss, my boi Airplane Charlie".*

Charlie couldn't do anything but salute Stone for the shout out. It was some broke niggas in the club looking like a million bucks. Charlie knew the next time he stepped out he had to be on point dress code and ice game. Rarri Game Mob Boss Charlie was failing that shit. He hugged so many hoes and shook so many niggas hands walking to the V.I.P. section. Standing there sipping out his cup, Charlie notice how deep Rarri crew was in the club. It was every bit of 40 of them females in all. Out the blue it seem like the whole club start yelling SQUAD, SQUAD, SQUAD, SQUAD, SQUAD…. It felt great to be the nigga he became.

Chapter 10 Wrapped In Duct Tape

After 5 ½ months of working his ass off in the streets, Charlie had stacked up about 280,000$. Not spending a dime period on shit except rental cars and food. His whole mind frame was saving up his money in case, he had to face more time (that was a big no, no to him).

Jose put Charlie on a plane to Oregon saying it was time to step it up a notch. This shit had to be big cause Charlie already had his biggest package dealing over 20 keys of cocaine and 300 pounds of some good popcorn mid. What else could they put on the table, no matter what it was he could handle it. Amari was waiting outside the airport for Charlie when the plane landed.

"Look Airplane when we get in front of Jose let me do all the talking".

"Man you tripping Rarri, whatever these folks talking bout I'm all ears my niggas".

"Nah this shit gon' go my way, I made you remember that".

(LOL) *"Folk stop trying me like I work for you my nigga. You just a runner, and on some real shit. Find you somebody to play with cause I'll do somethin' to yo ass. All that bullshit you be talking tell it to a nigga who want to hear it cause you got me all the way fucked up".*

Charlie walked off on that fool getting in side of the limousine. The driver took them to a big ass warehouse off of a dirt road. Jose and Ox was standing there waiting on them to pull up.

"Don't look like that grandson today is gon' be a bless day for you".

Jose rapped his arm around Charlie as they walked inside the building. The shit was duck off good from the road, inside there were tall ass plants everywhere of weed. The weed was loud as hell, it was surprising you couldn't smell the shit outside. Plants were hanging upside down on the left, some white men was clipping plants on the right and the rest of them was vacuum sealing the weed that was ready in pound bags.

It was every bit of 2,000 pounds in here, all kind of weed Purp, OG Kush, Granddaddy Purp, even White Rhino. Knowing loud was 66,000$ a pound, Charlie wanted to know how much of this shit he was about to get. Amari had a look on this face that was unexplainable. Jose took them all in the back of the warehouse to his office and rolled up four blunts all different kinds of weed. Passing everyone their own blunt before talking.

"Grandson; Ox and I flew you out here to show you that the things you have done for our organization these past few months are not being over looked. We appreciate everything, son. Things are better than ever right now. Every test that has been put in front of you, you have pass it with flying colors. Amari hasn't moved 500 pounds in a month as long as we been in business, and now he can handle a truck load. It doesn't take a rocket science to know you the cause of his success lately. So I'll be the one to say thank you for him. With that being said I'm willing to give you a chance of a life time. This loud situation is all yours if you want it. Take your time because it only grows once a year. 2,500 a pound. Ox will give you a better understanding later. Why are you looking like that son, is there a problem going on that I don't know about?"

"Nah pops, just this murder case I'm facing. I could do a lot more if I could get this shit from over my head. I want to marry Queen but don't want to end up leaving her out here by herself. Hell yeah, I love shawty".

"I'll handle that for you this week sometime, but when I do you owe me one, how bout that".

"If you take care of that for me you got a soldier for life swear".

"I'll update you in a few days".

They shook hands making the deal official.

Ox leaned over to Jose and said *"he want to marry our lil lady, we got to help him now."*

Charlie didn't understand how many cool points he got for telling them that. On the plane ride back home Ox called Charlie and told him that they were going to send him 100 pounds at a time. Really it was going to be 99 if he was going to keep 1 pound every time to smoke and Charlie had to pay for it. Ox had picked him over his own son. Ox could have gotten ten of them bitches cheap as that shit was.

On the plane Queen called and told Charlie she was in Atlanta, and to call her when he made it to Columbus. Her and lil Marc was going to Six Flags over Georgia. King hadn't answer the phone in 4 or 5 hours for Charlie and that wasn't like him. Last time they talked King said he was about to make a play with Lil Sosa, some nigga from Baker Village name Boom. Soon as the plane landed in Columbus Charlie went to the spot to see if King was in there sleep or something (on the Xanax bars like always). Pulling in the drive way Charlie saw Lil Sosa's Box Chevy in the yard. His blood pressure went up instantly. King knew better than to have anybody around the work. Charlie had made a memory note to slap the shit out of that nigga when he walked in the house.

The living room door was crack, that wasn't like King to leave the front door open. Charlie didn't have a gun on him so he didn't know what to expect when he got inside. The living room was clear, you could see blood all over the floor in the hallway, Lil Sosa was laying in the door way shot two times in the face (dead). Charlie knew the weed was gone, they didn't have any more dope. Charlie rush to the back looking for King. When he made it to the back bed room Charlie's heart dropped seeing King duct taped to a chair. His white tee all the way down to his shoes was covered in blood. King was barely breathing. Charlie ripped all the duct tape off of him and rushed him to the Medical Center ASAP. Charlie called Mrs. Jessie and told her King had been shot in the chest twice.

"Queen!"

"What's up bae".

"King just got shot he at the hospital in surgery".

"Come on Marc, we on our way bae".

Charlie knew he had to get Lil Sosa out the house. Feeling in his pockets finding the keys to his car. Charlie backed the car up to the bed room window out of sight. All that dead weight was heavy as a mufucker, it took everything he had to toss his body out the window. Blood from the body was all over Charlie, he took off the bloody clothes and threw them in the trunk with Lil Sosa. Queen was calling Charlie.

"Bae where you at?"

"What's up ma, where you at?"

"I'm at the hospital, where you at".

"Dam how fast were you driving, hold on I got a beep real quick".

It was Le'Kee mother Mrs. Tina

"Hello."

Marcus where you at.

"Just got back in town, something sound wrong".

"Have you done something to anybody lately? Is there a reason someone would want to hurt you or your family?"

"Ma what's going on? I haven't done shit to nobody".

"Somebody just killed Le'kee, and we can't find Lil Marc".

"What, dam man, fuck, I got Marc hewent to Six Flags with Queen, give me about 30 minutes I'll be over there".

Driving a car with a dead body in the trunk Charlie should have been more on point than he was. But his mind was racing trying to figure out who the hell had tried him like this. How the fuck did Lil Marc get with Queen in the first place.

It seem like going to Oregon fucking with Jose, Charlie had sold his soul to Illuminati or something. Le'kee was dead and King might be to. Charlie pulled in an abandon apartment building behind Wilson Apartment complex, and set the car on fire with Lil Sosa in it. It was fucked up how he had to do lil homie but for some reason Charlie knew that lil nigga had something to do with the 150 pounds that was missing and king getting shot.

Rarri Dynasty

Chapter 11 A Bag Of Money

Mary Tayler was the new district attorney over the Smith boy's case. Tomorrow was the big day for her, she was going to present the case to the grand jury after 16 long months. For the past three days she had been over looking every piece of the evidence. Knowing all three of the guys had good lawyers and Marcus had two, she had to be on top of her game. Mrs. Tayler called it a night early to get rest for tomorrow.

Dropping her purse at the door like normal, the front door closed on it's own. She notice a masked gun man standing there *"Don't make a sound."* Pointing towards the dining room with his AK47. Mary couldn't believe what was going on. She walked down the hallway to see her, 8 year old son, 16 year daughter and her husband Mike sitting at the dining table hand cuff to the chairs. They were sitting with duct tape over their mouths. Jose had a gun men to point at all their heads as he set at the far end of the table. Mary pissed on herself, it was like she was in a movie or something.

"Mary is there nothing you wouldn't do for you family?"

"There is nothing I wouldn't do for my family. Please do not hurt us I'll do anything".

"I told your family you are a great mother and wife. You are over a case, I'm sure you know who the Smith boys are?".

"Yes, I know them".

"Tomorrow is the day things getting serious, am I right?"

"Yes".

"This is how things are going to work, some kind of way you will let Marcus walk. I want all charges dismissed and the other two will plea out to something manageable. Or, I will kill your family in front of you. And you will have to live with the fact that the case meant more to you than your husband and kids".

"I'll do whatever, in the morning. I will go to them with a deal and Lord knows they will take it. And Marcus will never hear another word about this case".

Rarri Dynasty

"I'm a fair man Mrs. Tayler upstairs there is a bag with 75,000$ in it and a number to contact me. I expect to hear from you by noon".

Chapter 12 Throw His Momma Out The Plane

For the past three days Charlie had been riding around looking for Boom and Nurge. Trick was fucking the nigga baby momma, (on the low down bitch had gave them a picture of the clown). Charlie notice Lil Kobe when they turned into Baker village. Kobe was one of his lil homies that was going hard for the Gang in RYDC. Charlie told Nurge to pull over so he could holla at Kobe.

"What's up thug life? When did you get out Rarri?"

"Airplane my nigga, the man of the city, what it do Rarri?" You must got out today or something?"

"I got out yesterday big bra. I hear you ain't fucking with the south side. Nigga we Rarri over here to fool".

"You got to know I ain't rocking like that. You ready to put that mask down and get some money?"

"Hell nah, but I'm ready to put some work in if the check right. I heard yo baby momma got killed. Give me that job, I'll lay the whole city down".

" Keep your ears to the street for me bout that. I do have somethin' for you?.

"What dat?".

"You know a nigga name Boom?".

"Hell yeah, that lil bitch eating out here. He bout the only one of these niggas who gave me something when I got out. That nigga got them bags on deck".

"I bet he do, I'll give you 20 bands if you grab that fuckin' nigga. You don't even got to kill'em".

"Say Squad?"

"Squad shit, that's on everything. You get that nigga in less than 24 hours I'll make it 30 Rarri".

"Say no more, that nigga ain't from 14-40 for real anyway".

"That is my number lil bra, hit me up when you handle it".

"Fasho, his ass grass".

Sitting up at the hospital with King in a coma, Charlie bumped into Le'kees' Uncle Cook. Cook was an airplane instructor, who showed you the proper way to jump out of an airplane. He also was a pilot for hire by rich people. Charlie told Cook when he found out who killed Le'Kee he was going to throw their asses out of an airplane. Cook took it as a joke until Charlie told him he would give him 50,000$ to fly it for him. Cook told Charlie if it goes down, the door is behind him, he can't see shit up front.

Amari didn't come to the hospital not once, to see King in five days. Charlie had lost all the little respect he had left for that nigga. Mrs. Jessie never left King's side the whole time he was in the hospital. Sitting there talking to King like he did every right. King open his eyes for the first time. Charlie's phone rang; he never seen the number before.

"Yeah, who dis?"

"Big bra, what it do Rarri? This is Kobe, it only been 22 hours, I'm still in the running for them 30 right?"

"Hell yeah".

"What you want me to do with this bitch ass nigga?"

"You got a GPS on you phone right?"

"I should, it's a touch screen".

"636 6th ave apt. 2, meet me there in bout 15 minutes".

Charlie kissed King on the forehead and told him *"I told you I was gone get that fuck nigga bra"*

King cracked a little smile.

Walking out the room Mrs. Jessie was in the lobby getting some coffee. Charlie told her King had woke up.

"Marcus where are you going?".

"I'll be back I got to handle something real quick".

"Marcus please don't go kill anybody. You already got enough going on in your life right now son".

"I'll be back ma. I ain't bout to go do nothing like that".

Mrs. Jessie saw the look on his face; he was about to go do something crazy. Charlie was calling Cook as he got inside the elevator.

"Say Unk what's up with that first class flight we talked about?"

"What's up with that check we talked about nephew?"

"I'm bout to go count it up now".

"Well I'm bout to gas up then. Give me two hours tops".

Kobe was meeting Charlie at his spot. The same place it all went down at. Charlie wanted Boom to see the exact same thing King and Lil Sosa saw before he crossed them. Stopping to get the money Kobe had already made it to the spot. Charlie told him it was a spear key under the door mat. Kobe had his twin brother Cee with him. As Charlie walked in the house he could hear Boom saying *"Kobe why you doing this shit bra? I told you where the weed was lil homie."*

Charlie was wondering who the female was they had tied up with Boom.

"Who the fuck is that Kobe?"

"That nigga momma, the bitch was in the way. It was now or never and for 30 bands I like now, you feel me".

"I know that's right".

"What's up Cee?".

"Dat check all on my mind bra. You got to know it's Squad Life over here".

Charlie tossed Cee the bag with the money in it. His eyes lit up when he opened it and saw them 30 racks for real. Charlie asked them to follow him to the airport so the police couldn't get behind him in traffic while he was riding. Cook had just text Charlie and told him everything was a go. After loading both of them on the plane Cee wanted to ride too. Charlie told Kobe he should go too. Boom and his mom both was hog tied laying on their stomach with a pillow case over their heads. Kobe removed the pillow case from over Boom's head, when he realize he was on airplane Boom nut up.

"Charlie man, what the fuck y'all got going on?".

"You tell me, what you think next".

"Come on man, fuck that Mexican bra. We Boss my nigga GD- 74 till the world blow".

"Nigga I'm Rarri I ain't GD".

"Man let my momma live bra, she don't got nothin' to do with this shit. I'm who y'all want".

"Fuck that bitch, you didn't spear nobody why the fuck should we?".

As the plane got over Early County which is Blakely Georgia, Cook drop the latch to the door of the plane. *"Let's do it nephew while the cost is clear."*

With no hesitation what so ever Cee pushed Boom's momma out the plane.

Kobe grab Boom by the back of the shirt and told boom *"Squad nigga you ain't from Baker Village any way."* Throwing him out the plane.

Boom landed on top of the Early County jail and his mom landed in the parking lot on top of a squad car. When they made it back to Columbus and Charlie paid Cook the money he owed him. Cook told Charlie that he heard whoever killed Le'kee had a gold A6 Audi like the one Queen had.

Chapter 13 In Too Deep

Nobody had been arrested for Le'Kee murder. Her funeral was packed with people from the hood. Charlie did it big for her. Queen had a look or her face that Charlie couldn't understand. She looked sad as hell, the vibe was crazy because they didn't get along at all. The funeral cost 12,000$ cash because she didn't have any life insurance. Charlie kind of knew who did it but he wasn't 100% sure. Lil Marc moved in with Charlie.   They lived in a condo on the North Side out there with the white folks.   While unpacking Mr. Johnson, Charlie's lawyer called him with the best news ever.

"Mr. Smith I got some great news for you".

"What you got for me Mr. Johnson".

"Joel told the D.A. you didn't have anything to do with the murder. Both of your cousins are set up to take a plea next week on the 9th a 30 do 7. All the charges against you were dismissed this morning. You are lucky to have real friends

like you do son. Most young guys sell each other out. You stay out of trouble and if you ever need me again don't hesitate to call me'.

"Will do Mr. Johnson, will do".

King was released from the Medical Center after 19 days. He had lost a lot of weight laid up in that hospital bed. King let Charlie know Lil Sosa set him up, that made Charlie feel better for burning him up the way he did. King didn't know Boom had killed Lil Sosa. The weed was still coming in good, it was ugly on the cocaine at the moment, but Jose let them know everything would be back on point in about two weeks. King had been stressing that he had something he wanted to holla at Charlie about when the timing was right. Charlie showed King the two new spots and told him that if he ever showed another nigga he would kill him.

"Say bra my dad live in Miami Florida, he said the Rarri Gang big down that way. His name Hundo, he's one of the head MS13 down that way. He wants to meet you I told him you one of the niggas that started that Rarri shit".

"Man I don't even know anybody from Florida".

"My dad say it's a young Haitian cat name Yayo running shit. They use to be Zoe Pound now they claim Rarri Gang. He said they are killing and robbing everything moving down there in Dave County".

"Dam that's some crazy shit".

"Pop's said he got a package for me. His entire teem just got knocked off and he need my help right".

"Fasho when we leave?".

"Soon as ma go home we can head down there".

"Dats what's up".

Cee and Nurge had been grinding good, Queen had an Audi car so Charlie found a Q6 Audi truck. He painted it smoke gray and mounted it up on some 24 inch Davin. Queen felt it was too much, but hell Charlie felt his whole life was too much. Shit was going great for Charlie now especially since he found out he wasn't going back to jail. Hot and Trick had the city in the choke hold with the Loud, 4,000$ a pound, 250$ a zip they was doing every bit of 60 bands a week just selling Loud. The weed was that real gas.

Charlie had gotten infatuated with jewelry. Three rings on both hands, each one of the rings was no less than 4,000$. A presidential Rolex watch with a gray face that ran him 15,000$, and to set it off Charlie got a custom made 6 Karat diamond Rarri Gang necklace. The RG was big bold letters flooded with diamonds. At the bottom of the chain said "Squad Life Or No Life". Charlie and Queen both had new gold teeth in their mouth. Charlie made a statement in the city with his ice game, it spelled out he was getting real money. He was the King of the C-Town.

Eight days later King was ready to go see his father. He didn't want his mother to know; for some reason. King said growing up his mother didn't let him fuck with his father period after they broke up. It was something to do with Jose and his grandfather on his dad's side. Looking at gang land on T.V. Charlie knew them MS13 megos didn't play so he had Nurge and Kobe with him just in case. Charlie already felt he had to go see the Yayo nigga down there reppin his shit. Because it wasn't but one Rarri Gang and he was the Boss.

Miami was a beautiful ass city, Columbus didn't have nothing on Miami. Even the females looked better, and it was way more niggas getting money down this way. Summer just had jumped off so the women was walking around with hardly anything on. Hundo told them to meet him at his Strip club called Golden Cats. At 3:00 in the afternoon the Hummer 2 they rode in what might have been the cheapest car in the parking lot. You had to be on a

V.I.P. list to even get in the club. King called his father and Hundo sent some mego to the door to let them in. Charlie wasn't sure if he was in a strip club or a hoe house. Every bitch in the building was super bad. Nothing over 120 pounds, those hoes didn't have on anything (no shoes, not even a ribbon to hold their hair up). Walking to the back of the club Mego's with guns were everywhere. You could tell Hundo was running shit for real when they all made it in the room, Hundo told one of his goons that he didn't have to pat them down they was La familia.

"Son how was the flight?".

"(laughing) Man let's just handle business cause you are far from a father".

"*Amari is far from a father, as is that punta you call a grandfather. I was forced out your life for a falling out between my father and Jose. So if you want to leave be my guess, but I'll be dam if you sit here and disrespect me son or not*".

As Hundo started raising his voice every Mego in the room stood up and pointed their guns at us. King was on some other shit. Seeing how fast Hundo got mad, Charlie knew it was a lot of shit going on King didn't know nothing about. Staring at king, Hundo waved his hand and they all lower their guns. Hundo started speaking in Spanish, but before he could get 6 good words out King stopped him.

"*Charlie is my right hand man so with all due respect he needs to know what's being said*".

"*Well he needs to learn fuckin Spanish then*".

"*Man I'm gonna let y'all handle this shit, me and my people going to wait outside*".

"*They need to wait outside but you need to stay*".

Kobe and Nurge got up to walk out the room, Kobe looked back at Charlie before he exited the room. Charlie shook his head letting him know he was ok.

"So you are Charlie Rarri, the leader of the Rarri Gang? I thought you was from Overtown".

"Nah I'm from Downtown".

"So how did it reach all the way down here?".

"I haven't the slightest idea".

"I here Ice is taking over GA. I want y'all to push my work for me up there. Become a team, build a bond, maybe become a family".

"What's the numbers on that shit?".

"8,000$ a pound, best ticket in the country".

"So how many pounds you talking about at one time?".

"I don't know, we don't be fuckin with that shit. I wouldn't say no more than 15 or 20".

"That's perfect".

"Long as I don't have to be responsible for getting it back home I'm down. What about you King?".

"That's alright price, but Columbus got some of the purest meth I've ever seen so for that ticket it needs to be A1".

"This is the best of the best".

"That's what we need".

Hundo was a real Boss, Charlie told him they was going to Overtown to check on this Rarri Gang shit. He made sure they had guns to take with them.

When King got in the truck Charlie said *"Best meth you ever seen"* King bust out laughing.

King knew, Charlie knew his ass never seen meth a day in his life better yet in Georgia. Overtown had to be one of the worst looking neighborhoods Charlie had ever seen. Overtown made B.T.W. look like the suburbs. Kids walking around with no shoes on, crack heads was everywhere. Shit was fucked up. They had niggas standing on top of every building, these niggas was ready for war. It wasn't a person in the entire neighborhood including the females that didn't wear a gray and black bandana tied around there heads. These niggas was reppin Rarri Gang harder than anybody in Columbus. The young niggas was tying the flags around the front of their pants to hold them up like a belt.

This shit was serious in Overtown. RG4L [Rarri Gang 4 Life] and Squad Life or No Life was written everywhere. Whoever Yayo was they had to fuck with homes the long way. Nurge pulled up on a young nigga that couldn't have been know older than 12 or 13, Charlie rolled the window down to holla at him.

"Say lil nigga! you know who is Yayo?"

"Nigga fuck you. You betta' get from round here before somethin' happen to yo ass".

"Like what lil nigga?".

The young light skin nigga was sitting on the bike reached in his pants. Kobe already had his window rolled down. The lil nigga was fumbling so bad he drop the gun when he saw Kobe hang out the window with that Teck 9.

"Lil pussy ass nigga don't die before you get some pussy."

"Nigga kill me! Real Rarri niggas don't see 18 anyway. I ain't scared that's on King Charlie".

"Nigga I am Charlie".

Charlie stepped out the truck and took off his shirt so the young nigga could see the tattoos he got in Eastman. [Squad Life C-Town 80's Baby] it took up his whole chess.

Lil homie knew it was him when he read Rarri Gang across his stomach.

"My bad OG. Come on gangst , I'll show you where big homie them at".

Pulling into the dead end- it was a group of niggas standing on a porch. Lil bubby got out the truck and yelled *"Yayo"* when the big nigga stood up Kobe spotted him off the rip.

"Charlie that's big boy. We was in Milledgeville RYDC with him".

"What that nigga name is?".

"Umm umm".

"He was yo cellmate Rarri".

"Tory James, that's that nigga name".

"Dam sho' is".

Rarri Dynasty

Everybody got out the truck, when the niggas on the porch seen the big ass gun Kobe had they all started walking backwards point their guns at them. Yayo notice who it was and went ham "put that shit down nigga that's King Charlie" Yayo looked happy as a mufucker to see Charlie. Yayo hit Charlie with a hand shack that never seen before. Yayo was flagged up to. In RYDC Yayo wasn't nothing, he always said in Fla, his name held weight. Niggas know how it go when you locked up in another state, shit be a lil ugly for you. Yayo wasn't even Rarri down the road but he for real with this shit out here. It seem like the whole hood was anxious to meet Charlie. Yayo pulled Charlie to the side so they could talk.

Big homie what brings you all the way down here.

They say the Rarri Gang turnt up down here, you know I had to come check it out.

We just trying to make a name for our self.

I see y'all done did that. So you the man out here hun.

Never that you the king, I just run my city Airplane.

Y'all niggas ready to get some real money Rarri.

"*Fuck yeah. Pull wrote me one time and told me y'all was in the C-Town eating. I been trying to run my check up to show you what we had going on down this way*".

"*What's that young nigga name that just got out the truck with us*".

"*Who you talking about Dirty Redd*".

"*Yeah him. This what we bout to do, you and lil homie gone go back with me, I'm gone seed you back down here with some work to see what's up. I got a lil weed and some Ice for you*".

"*Meth is where the money at*".

"*I want you to turn that lil young nigga up right there*".

"*When you gone be ready to go*".

"*I'm ready now, we bout to jump on the plane right now and dip. But lesson ya'll got to clam down for real, the mego I fuck with really want to do some to you. So chill so we can get this money, you feel me*".

"*Fasho big bra*".

Rarri Dynasty

Yayo had a real movement going on that Charlie wanted in on. He had some real young niggas in his circle, and Charlie liked that young nigga Dirty Reed for some reason. Charlie road Yayo around the city and to show the type of money he was getting. He educated him about building a lil army and the limitless possibilities he could accomplish in a short period of time.

Charlie sent Yayo back with 16 ounces of Ice, 10 pounds of gas and 50 pounds of mid all Yayo had to do was drive safe and make it home and it was on. Charlie didn't feel he would fuck over him, but if he did Kobe was gone be on the first thing smoking to Dave County to off his ass.

Chapter 14 Mexican Mafia

Charlie flag the C-Town after seeing what Yayo and his click had going on. Using Facebook Charlie started networking with all the niggas who was rocking with him in RYDC from Atlanta to Macon. Charlie couldn't keep enough cocaine between him and Yayo. Jose couldn't believe how fast Charlie was flying that shit. (30 keys a week wasn't shit to get off of). Charlie had ran through all 3,500 pounds of the loud Jose had; It took 4 months.

Shit was better than ever in the street, but at home Queen was ready to get married. Charlie wasn't ready for all that; Queen and Lil Marc had a strong bond. Charlie believe in his heart she had something to do with Le'Kee getting killed. Charlie didn't fuck with her, Charlie wasn't about to forget she killed his sons momma. He blamed himself for Le'Kee's death.

Rarri Dynasty

Pull lil times was flying by down the road for him. Pull was on his Rarri Gang shit bad. The whole prison knew he was Charlie right hand man and the Rarri Gang was controlling the streets of Columbus. Pull had done played under a lady officer down there in Macon State Prison were we was, she was bring him in 4 pounds of loud at a time. That nigga was making like 2,500$ off each pound. Now this fool wanted to get 4 and 5 ounces of Ice to every drop. The lil fat hoe didn't want nothing but 1,000$ every time to bring the shit in the jail.

Kobe and lil Cee had the city on smash. Some lil young nigga from the East Side had ran off on Kobe with 2 zips of hard and lil bra was rocking like it was a brick or something. Kobe was on the run bad for doing a drive by and killing two of the niggas lil homies and shooting the nigga sister. Charlie tried to tell Kobe lil ass to chill out. Kobe said he was into deep and he had to kill lil buddy so the nigga couldn't testify against him in court. King was starting to get beside himself now that he was seeing a lil bit of money.

"Say plane you forgot to put that money in the stash didn't you bra?"

"Nah, I got it with me bra".

"I'm just checking cause you didn't put that lil change in there for that pound this morning".

"Nigga I got that lil money with me now, don't be calling me like you checking me fool".

"Man here we go, I'm just trying to make sure my check right".

"Yo check, nigga don't get beside yourself".

"I can't get beside myself bout my shit, that weed money I put it where it go every time. You need to do the same thang".

"Fasho my nigga, sell that shit yo self next time lame ass nigga and make sure you get that shit out my spot before the day over with cause you don't pay know bills in there".

(LOL) "You ain't said nothing but a word nigga".

Rarri Dynasty

King was running with some lil fake ass MS13 niggas off the Midside of town in a lil trailer park. They had him feeling his self. Only reason Charlie wasn't gone get that nigga killed was because he had too much love for Mrs. Jessie. She was already staying with Queen and Charlie ever sense she caught Amari cheating on her again. This was how the game go doe the nigga you fuck with the long way will cross you out every time. But karma was a bitch, that hoe will come back and bit you in the ass 9 times out of 10 when you fuck over a good nigga.

Chapter 15 First Plane Smoking

"Jose I'm just calling to let you know both of your grandsons are running Ice from Fla to GA for Hundo and his people".

"What? Amari is this something you heard or know".

"Both, I told my father I guess he over looked it. But it's true I'm sure of this".

"Amari if I find out you're lying, I will did with you".

"Let me handle this for you Jose, I know Airplane wasn't who we thought we was".

"I'll handle it; me and Marcus are going to have a sit down one on one. I feel the only reason you telling me this is out of hatred".

The BET Hip Hop Awards was held in Atlanta every year. Charlie took his whole team with him and their old ladies. The Rarri Gang was about to go ball out for the weekend. They were 25 deep on the red carpet. Third row seats, back stage passes, the whole nine yards.

Queen wore a sleeveless, tight fitting Louis Vuitton dress with the heels to match. Small LV's all over the dress and shoes. The dress was green with black and gray LV's on it.

The Ferrari 599 GTB Fiorano that Queen was driving was matching her dress as well, hunter green with a white top with white interior. Charlie was killing the red carpet with the velour suit he had on made out of turtle, 17,000$ outfit. The carpet was full with rappers, movie stars, the works. Rocko Da Don stopped Charlie to ask him who design his clothes. A.J. from the show 106 and Park stopped Queen to ask her about the dress she was wearing. Free was co-host for the show. She put the mic to Queen's mouth to ask her what her name was. Before she could speak two gun shots went off BOOM, BOOM. Kobe pulled out his gun and four more shots rang out BOOM, BOOM, BOOM, BOOM, Charlie seen Queen fall. Charlie looked up from the ground as Yayo stood over him trying to help him up.

(yelling) *"Rarri don't die on me man."*

Charlie passed out in Yayo's arms. Nurge and Kobe had Queen trying to make it to the truck.

Kobe was in the truck talking crazy, *"Yayo, if I find out"*.

"Find out what nigga, you better miss me with that fuck shit you talking Kobe".

"These niggas done popped my nigga".

"It's that bitch ass nigga King man, I'm telling you Kobe. I know King lil bitch ass, he wouldn't do his sister like that. That nigga a hater, he trying to get Charlie out the picture bra".

Grady Hospital was the close by. Cee had his Porsche Truck wide open on the expressway. Charlie got hit breaking his collar bone, and in the right leg. Queen was hit in the arm. The gun man had to be far as hell. He hit them with a .223 built and didn't kill them or he was a bad shooter.

The surgery took 13 hours on Charlie. He had lost a lot of blood. Queen recovered quickly. Charlie needed a blood transfusion, he was still on life support.

Rarri Dynasty

The FBI was all over the hospital, they wanted to know who in the hell Charlie was and who wanted to take him out like that. The Feds knew they would try again. None of this shit was adding up to Charlie. Kobe saying it's Yayo and his crew. Yayo saying it was King. He felt they should just start killing everybody. Jose would have a car waiting on Charlie whenever he was released. Charlie knew the shooter wasn't in his family, but whoever it was their ass was going to be on the first plane smoking.

Chapter 16 Sleepless Nights

Life was a roller coaster ride for Charlie at the moment he didn't know who to trust. He wasn't sure who had a hit out on him and Queen. Charlie had his guard up. His bet was on King. His mind was telling him King had something to do with the shooting because Charlie felt he had forgot what loyalty was. Charlie didn't want to do anything stupid because he had too much to lose including Queen, Lil Marc and 4 million dollars he had saved up.

Jose had been trying to get Charlie to Texas for the last month but Charlie didn't trust him either. The cocaine and weed didn't make it in like it was suppose to and Charlie didn't have a choice but to see Jose and find out what he wanted. Charlie sent Cee, Kobe, Yayo and Nurge three days ahead of time, than booked a flight to Dallas. Charlie knew them four niggas there would walk through hell and hot water for him. King called Charlie time he landed in T.X., they had not talked in a few weeks.

Squad.

"Charlie, we got a problem bra".

"Oh bra, I'm bra again cause we got a problem?"

"Bra the van with the Ice in it got carjacked".

"Who the fuck knew about the ice?   "I didn't know about the shipment date".

"Nobody knew about the shit.   The bad part about it is; the van got jacked in Georgia so Hundo saying it's on us".

"Us or yo ass? Ain't no us in that shit!"

"Come on bra, you know I don't have that type of money for 50 pounds. If I did I wouldn't even be calling you Charlie".

"Look Rarri, that's yo problem not mine. You need to hang up and call me when you handle that shit. Tell Hundo I don't owe him shit".

"So you just gon' leave me out here in the water to drown bra?"

{Click the phone hung up in King's Face}

When Charlie got off the phone with King he text Dirty Redd and told him to keep an eye on Hundo in case that nigga tried some bullshit. Dirty Redd text back Fasho big homie. Jose lived in a big ass glass house, this shit was made like a skybox inside the Atlanta Hawks game or something. Jose house was a player's dream. Charlie had a nice crib but this mufucker was show stopping. For the average nigga from B.T.W. you only see shit like this on TV. The back of the house was like looking off a mountain top.

"Your eyes tell me you like what you see son" said Jose *proudly".*

"Yeah, this bitch nice".

"A man with your money and power Charlie should enjoy life more".

"I know what it's like to have nothing, life is great for me", replied Charlie.

"Marcus, I took you from a jail cell to a kingpin, from a corner hustler to a made man all across Georgia and you go behind my back and make deals without me?"

"Jose, I never asked you for anything. You did this on the strength of your granddaughter. And secondly, I didn't go behind yo back and do shit".

"So this Ice thing is made up? Amari told me everything Marcus".

"I don't got nothing to do with that shit. That's some shit King and his daddy got going on. But I did go up there to make sure shit worked out right for lil bra and Hundo. Make sure they didn't try and get over on him".

"So you never made a red cent off none of these deals?" *Jose said with an attitude.* (Deep inside he did not want to start doubting the man he came to love for his granddaughter)

"Man I'm a real street nigga. Yeah, I made some money off that shit. If it's a cap in the shit I want in, but really all these questions are irrelevant cause I have never been a dime short or day late with your money. So is this the reason you got me shot?" (Charlie was mad but he managed to hold his temper in check)

"Why would I get you and my only granddaughter shot?

And if I order the hit you would be dead. You told me if took care of your court case I had a soldier for life. So I'm asking my soldier to stop doing business with the Mexican Maifa. Hundo is a snake his father is a snake, so is king. It's in their bloodline", said Jose in a fatherly t1one.

"I just told you, I don't have nothing to do with them MS13 mufuckers. I need to know who the hell shot me and my wife".

(Jose gesture for Charlie to sit down in a chair in front of him). *"What I am about to tell you should never leave this room. I am about to betray a long time loyal friend that I love like a brother".*

(Charlie sat down as he was instructed. He felt close to Jose and respected him as a boss and father) *"I ain't gone do no talking. I'm just gon' take action".*

"Amari order the hit and he didn't have any permission from me or Ox".

Charlie face showed no emotions. He had so many questions in his head, but he could only stare at the man in front of him. Why would he let someone shoot at his granddaughter and not take a hit on them immediately? Bullshit.

Charlie knew exactly what he needed to do and he didn't need orders from anyone to do it. He lost all respect for Jose the moment he said he knew who tried to kill him.

Queen had a lil cousin name Soulja in Charlotte who Charlie had been fronting weed for a lil min. Charlie told Soulja to take care of Amari for him and don't speak on it. Charlie didn't want Queen or Mrs. Jessie to know he had something to do with it. Charlie didn't even tell Kobe what he was about to do. Jose was on Charlie's shit list too once he found a new plug. He was gone kill his ass too.

The streets was afraid of Kobe, Charlie was about to put fear in the world. Charlie was out for revenge. Mufuckers better beware cause he was more ruthless now than ever before.

Pull was telling Charlie to turn up on these niggas, the next thing he was gon' be saying was turn down bra. Charlie had a list and mufuckers was about to turn up missing. Hundo was next on the list. He had life all fucked up.

"Airplane Charlie".

"What it do pimp?"

"I'm sure you know there was a problem with the package.

What I don't understand is, you know my number when there is a problem, but I don't hear from yo ass when shit going good".

"I told you once it makes it to Georgia it's yours. I know you love your son so I need that money ASAP".

"Whatever you gon' do, do it my nigga cause I swear on my son grave I ain't giving yall mego's shit. You got me all fucked up with yo punk ass son".

"Listen nigger that's 600,000$ that ya'll owe me. If I don't get my money in three weeks I'm killing both of ya'll", Hundo said with his hand under his t-shirt and in his pants.

Charlie didn't flinch. He knew this bitch as nigga wasn't about to draw a gun on him. He wouldn't have a chance in the world to go up against Charlie's quick trigger finger.

Rarri Dynasty

"Fuck you wet back."Do what you do, pussy ass nigga".
(Charlie was about to kill Hundo right there on the spot, but he managed to keep his cool).

Yayo put an APB out on Hundo and Mia for 20 racks every lil Rarri in Overtown is on the look out for that fool. He ain't gon' last a week, with them lil bad ass Haitian niggas looking for him.

Chapter 17 No Charlie, Please!

King stupid ass had let Hundo and the weak ass MS13 niggas play right under him. They use King to learn the in and outs of Columbus and didn't need him anymore. Hundo sent about 12 of his own megos to Columbus. King got his own spots in South Park Mobile Homes. King thought everything was sweet since he had 3 traps doing numbers, but his shit was a setup from day one to cross his ass out. King realize some shit was in the game. He didn't have any work, but his lil cousin Hundo sent up there did. He told Charlie what was going on. Charlie told him don't worry he had a trick for all that.

Amari set seat at the red light down town Charlotte on the corner West 26 and Trade st, riding in yellow and brown Camaro. Amari was slipping had with the top down on his convertible with music blasting. He didn't even see the green minivan pull up on the side of him. The passenger of the van rolled the window down, getting Amari's attention.

"You want to sell it".

Amari tried to turn the music down. Before he could look back up and respond, the back door of the van sled open. Two niggas with mask on jumped out shooting. BANG, BANG, BANG, BANG, BANG, BANG, BANG, BANG, BANG, BANG, BANG,

They fired every shot out both guns, the M-16 with 75 rounds and the AR-15 with a 100 round drum on it. Amari got hit everywhere all in the head, face, chess the car didn't even get hit too many times. Soulja was on the passenger side of the van. Once the niggas in the back stop shooting, he got out of the car and emptied his 38 in Amari's face BANG, BANG, BANG, BANG, BANG, BANG. Charlie told Soulja to make sure he was dead so that's exactly what he did.

One thing about Mexicans when they move it's not just one coming. They ride deep. Charlie knew he had to make the first move. Charlie sent his young boys from B.T.W. to South Park 8 cars deep, 4 in each car and told them to air that bitch out. Dam near 25 young niggas shooting Mac 11's and Mac 90's. Jose felt Charlie had started a cartel war, telling him he needed to get out of town. Charlie wasn't trying to hear that shit. The CNN NEWS said 23 Mexican were killed in the shooting, 17 of them were kids, 46 people in all was shot. A week after the trailer park shooting; Kobe was missing for a few day but that was normal for him, he called Charlie to talk to him.

"If you want sum'in done right, you got to do it yourself. What you want me to do with this fuck nigga Hundo Charlie, kill'em?"

"Put that bitch in the trunk and bring him back Rarri".

"Fasho Squad".

Charlie knew exactly what he wanted to do with that sissy, he called Cook

"Say unc' I need you man".

"What's up Marcus."

:I need one of them first class flights again".

"Money funny right now, so long as everything, everything than everything gone be everything you feel me".

"Come on unc' everythings everything".

"It will have to be tomorrow night".

"That's cool unc".

"I'll call you when I'm ready for you nephew".

"Fasho unc' say no more".

Mrs. Jessie was taking the death of her husband hard. After moving out from the house with Queen and Charlie, she got her on place in Columbus at some apartments called the Lakes. While Charlie was waiting on the Squad to make it to town with Hundo, he went to see his mother in law. She had been on his mind a lot, knowing it was all his fault. Charlie knocked on the door when Mrs. Jessie opened the door she had a big smile on her face, she didn't say anything, just walked off letting Charlie in headed back to the kitchen. She poured two cups of VSOP Remy the white kind, Charlie had turn her on to Remy. This was the only kind of liquor he drank white Remy. For some odd reason she couldn't stop smiling.

"Hey Marcus, what brings you over here?".

"Just checking on you Mrs. Jessie, how you holding up".

"Call me mom for the 20 millionth time, and yes son. I'm at peace. It's been a long time sense I been free, I feel 17 again".

"What you mean you feel free ma?   I don't understand".

"You really want to hear my problems Marcus or should I say Charlie, Airplane that is?"

"Come on Mrs. Jessie what's that all about?"

"Marcus I just wanted my kids to be happy. Do you know how happy I was when we found out Queen couldn't have kids, so she wouldn't have to ever go through what I did? Son my father should have been a pimp instead of a kingpin cause he sold me coming up to be the man he is today. I never knew what it was like to experience real love. I had sex with two men only to build a bond, to make our families strong. You know why I care for you so much Marcus?"

I thought I saw tears coming to Ms Jesse's eyes as she continued to talk.

"Nah, but I want to know".

"I know you truly care for my child. To overlook her killing the mother of your child, knowing it was an accident. I know the love you have for her is real. Promise me you won't let power and fame go to your head".

"I promise".

"I want you to know I know what you did, Queen knows as well, we all know. And she's not mad at you, so marry her Marcus, and treat her like the Queen she is son'.

Mrs. Jessie was right, Charlie went to the mall and found Queen a ring for 6,000$ and start trying to come up with a way to pop the big Question. Charlie always knew Queen had something to do with Le'Kee getting killed. He wanted to ask her but knowing what he had done to Amari he couldn't. Pulling in the drive way a Atlanta number called Charlie.

"Hello".

"Hello, I'm looking for Mr. Smith, is this him".

"May I ask who I'm speaking to please".

"Mr. Hardy, from the Board of Pardons and Parole. I'm trying to check address for Jody Smith:.

"What address did he give you sir?"

"2200 Sureway Court".

"Yes that's my house".

"So it's ok for him to parole out there?".

"Yes. Is he about to come home or is this just a random call or something?".

"Yes, he's about to come home. I am about to fax his paperwork off now. You can be looking for him within 6 to 8 weeks, maybe less".

Charlie was real happy his boy was about to get out. Pull had been locked up for 41 months. Queen open the door for Marc they haven't been on the best terms, but maybe things would change when he asked her to be his wife. When she open the door Charlie grabbed her by the neck like he was mad and pushed her up against the wall.

"You think I'm crazy don't you? You think I'm going to let you get away from me without--

(Queen was balled up) saying *"I'm sorry, bae please don't hit me"*; her eyes was close she didn't even see Charlie get down on one knee). *Without being my wife"*

Tears started to flow down her face.

"Queen, I know I have done a lot of fucked up shit in the past and so have you, but I want to be with you for the rest of my life. Will you marry me".

"Marcus I didn't mean to kill her I swear. I pulled the gun out and she rushed me. I can't even sleep at night. It's so hard to look at Ja'Marcus".

"You don't have to explain".

"Yes I do; she was following me and I pulled over to see what she wanted. She was mad that your sister let Lil Marc go with me. We started fighting and ended up on the ground. I got up real quick and got the gun out you gave me. I told her to chill before I shoot her ass. She picked up a brick up off the ground and said;("you gone have to shout me than Bitch") and charged me with the brick. I close my eyes and shot the gun three times. Lil Marc never woke up, he stayed sleep in the back seat of the car. I didn't

try to kill her Marcus, you have to believe me".

"I believe you bae"; Charlie said with tears in his eyes.

Charlie held Queen as she cried in his arms. The good thing was Lil Marc didn't see his mother get killed, so that meant they wouldn't ever have to tell him.

Chapter 18 Shoot'em Up Bang!

Cook and Charlie was standing in front of the plane when Yayo and Kobe pulled up. You could tell something was bothering them both, Yayo stepped out the Ford Focus holding his stomach throwing. The smell that was coming out the car when Charlie walked up was unbearable.

Kobe what the fuck that smell is Rarri.

Man Yayo been farting for the last two, three hours bra.

Nigga that's yo nasty ass, with that bullshit not me.

Charlie open the trunk and the smell almost killed him. Hundo had passed out from the smell back there. The other mego they had in the trunk with Hundo had gotten so scared, he had a heart attack and died. The nigga had shitted and pissed all over his self. Yayo asked Charlie what they was gone do with the other nigga. Charlie already knew what he was getting at, Yayo didn't fuck with them planes. That fool was scared of heights. Charlie told

Yayo to do whatever he wanted with that clown. Loading Hundo on the plane, Charlie could hear him trying to say something through the duct tape. Kobe took the tape off his mouth after they got him on the plane. You know a person will say anything when their life is on the line.

"Airplane please don't kill me man".

"Why not give me one good reason why I shouldn't".

"Cause you will have a war on your fucken hands. Do you know who my father is".

"Fuck yo daddy, I'm built for war. Put the tape back on that bitch mouth".

"Wait, wait, umm, umm".

"Let him talk Rarri".

"I just got a truck load in Charlie, you can have it all".

"How much is in the truck".

"More Ice then you ever seen. 500 pounds or pure Ice, do you know what kind of money that is. I'll get missing you will never see me again".

"Where is it?"

"I'll take you to it".

"Where is it?"

"Let me take you Airplane".

"I'll call someone and direct them to the truck, or fuck it I got money".

"Y'all might kill me anyway".

"Open the door unk, fuck that wet back throw him out lil bra".

"Wait Charlie hold up".

"What you waiting on Kobe throw that nigga out".

"927 Brick yard Rd. Mia, please don't kill me you can have it all".

Charlie looked at Kobe with the most serious look ever "he still talking, throw that fool out" Kobe had Hundo by the back of the shirt moving slow, Kobe wanted to check on the work first. This was the lick of a life time.

Charlie jumped up out his seat and grabbed Hundo by the back of his belt "NO CHARLIE PLEASE!" and tossed his ass right out the plane. Hundo's body landed in the middle of traffic on to I-85.

Charlie we should have checked on that work first bra.

That nigga could of sent us to a set up bra. If it's there it's there, if not fuck it, it is what it is. To be a Boss you got to thank like one Rarri.

Charlie gave Dirty Reed the address to the house where the 18 wheeler was supposed to be. Dirty Redd called back about 15 min later and said the truck was there, back in on the side of a house.

"Keep yo' eyes on it we on the way baby boy."

Cook dropped Charlie and Kobe off at the airport in Florida. Yayo had set the other Mexican up in the front seat of the Ford Focus, in front of the government center, right before court started. Leaving a not on the window seal that said {SQUAD LIFE or NO LIFE}

Rarri Dynasty

Charlie had never seen so many pounds in his whole life that he didn't have to pay a dime for. Charlie played the game safe he left all the work in Mia so they wouldn't take any chances of getting knocked off trying to drive it back home. Kobe was on fire back home so he stayed if Fla to chill and to keep his eye on Yayo, Charlie didn't need that nigga trying to turn into Tony Montana, you know howblack folks get. Charlie Split the 500 pounds up with Yayo, Kobe and Dirty Redd to prove his loyalty to the Squad. If he made sure everybody had money than none of them would ever cross him out for it. The shit was free anyway, might as well bless the team with it.

After 46 long months Pull was released from prison. Queen drove down the road to pick him up. Pull knew Charlie was getting money, but seeing was believing. Pull was in the car with Queen and Lil Marc when they pulled up in the projects. The whole hood was outside in B.T.W. waiting on Pull to pull up like the boss he was. Pull got out the Audi truck big as hell 6'4 240 solid, waves spinning like a fool. Soon as he saw Charlie he hugged him picking him up off of his feet.

"Nigga put me down fool".

"Plane don't make me knock you out in front of all these folks now, (laughing)".

"Don't get killed bra, enjoy your freedom, life good out here".

"I forgot you was the king round here cuz".

"And don't forget it soulja".

{Pull gave Charlie some dap and another hug}

That's on the Squad I won't bra.

Charlie toss Pull a set of keys and told him to follow him to the parking lot. Pull couldn't believe his eyes a Midnight Blue BMW 760, on some 26 inch DUB's. Pulled hit the up lock button on the car "Dam y'all turnt up bad like this" Pull saved up almost 40 racks in jail, but when he open the shoe box on the driver seat floor his eyes almost popped out his head.

"Plane how much fucken money this is Rarri?".

"250,000$ my nigga. Shit real out here, I keep telling you".

"Bra, what am I suppose to do with all this shit? Hold on to it or something?"

"I don't give a fuck what you do with it my nigga. Go to the Foxy Lady and fuck it up. We got dump trucks of that shit bra".

Chapter 19 No Disrespect

In two weeks flat Pull had got the whole gang under a real Structure. Charlie was the General, Pull was the Caption, Kobe was the Lieutenant over GA and Yayo was the LT. over Florida. King was the head stash house operator. He over all the stash houses Charlie had over in Phenix City, Alabama. Charlie had forgot about a lot of the lil' niggas from the hood. He stop traveling down there to check up on them, he had put others in charge of overseeing what went on that side of town.

Pull came home and put all the ass on his team, Pull was like Nino Brown to them young niggas. Charlie didn't even sell hard know more, but soon as Pull got his 6 bricks he cooked them all up. Putting young niggas in spots all around down town. They had a trap in the horse shoe on 3rd, right across from Lil Joes Liquor Store going ham. They wasn't selling nothing but rocks. Splade, Bilo and Ben had that booming, with that straight drop glass. Fucking with Pull in a matter of three months, it wasn't a hood in the city getting off like Down Town, from 8th street back to 1st Ave. Pull was the only one who could keep Kobe lil crazy ass under control.

Only thing the Squad was missing now was Fatty. Pull made sure Charlie wasn't hands on with the work anymore, all Charlie had to do was count money and make sure it got to the plug the was gone handle the rest. On the low Charlie had picked up a real bad gambling habit.

Cook hook Charlie up with a rich white friend name Floyd Goodson who sold him a nice mini jet for 600 grand. Charlie and Queen started taking trips all over the world. Europe was the first place they went. Queen always wanted to go there. She wanted to go to Mexico too, where her mother and grandfather were born. Charlie made it happen for her. He always wanted to go to California. After going to a beach in Kelly, Charlie went to the slums of Oakland and met a Crip nigga name Ducc who was getting 10 Bricks. In no time, Charlie was going back and forth serving Ducc. He would buy 10 and Charlie would put 5 on top of what he was buying. Fucking with Ducc and his home boy Mail Man, Charlie was making big moves all across the west coast.

Everybody was ready for the wedding, Mrs. Jessie rented out the Civic Center, across the street from B.T.W. for 20 racks. The Civic Center held 14,000 people, they didn't have close to that many folks coming but it was going to be thick. Pull was the best man, the whole wedding was gray and black. The wedding was a slick concert on the low, Ducc, Pull, and Yayo chipped in to bring both of Queen's favorite singers to the wedding Keyshia Cole and Monica. They were deep inside Charlie's dressing room Trick, Dirty Redd, Hot. Pull walked in with a book bag on his back and told everybody to stand up. Pull started patting everyone down.

"What the fuck you doing nigga?" Kobe asked him.

Charlie started to get upset, he didn't know what type of shit pull was going on.

"Nigga get the fuck up out of here like we done stole something from you or something. You tripping nigga".

I'm tripping, y'all niggas slipping it's bout 6,000 people out there, Mexicans and all".

"It's a fucking concert, wedding Pull. What do you expect fool?"

"Y'all niggas must be green or something. Ain't none of y'all niggas strapped. Nigga didn't you get shot at the BET Awards? What the fuck make today any different?. Get married Rarri don't get killed fool".

Pull was right you never know where this shit will go down at. Inside the bag Pull had was holsters and glock 9mm for everybody. On top of that Pull told Charlie Kobe, Cee,

Jack, and Zax was spaced out in the crowd with Mac 11's if anything funny come about. Charlie was happy to have Pull out here with him, he couldn't take no more of them bullets, them bitches hurt. Pull even put a 380. In the back part of Charlie waste band.

As the wedding began and everyone started to take their seats, Charlie notice a puzzled look on King's face. King was the ring man. Charlie was having a hard time trying to remember his values. Looking around Charlie saw Jose, his mother, father, and Mrs. Jessie, once Ox started walking down the ill with Queen, Charlie started trying to get right. "Get it together man" Charlie told his self.

Because of you now I really understand what real love is. When I was down you pick me up, now that I'm up I won't you down. It takes a hell of a women to full your shoes. And if your willing to spend the rest of your with me that means your prepared for the worst. That's the only type of person I'll give my last name to. Queen I love you with all my heart.

It took Charlie a second to get it together but when he did, it worked out right. The preacher stood up and spoke.

If any one feels these two shouldn't be wed in holy matrimony speak now or forever hold your peace.

Right then about 20 Mexicans stood up holding guns. They was all spaced out in two's. The Mexican on the front row standing buy his self, pulled out a two 357. Charlie notice what was about to go on and pushed Queen out the way. Next thing you know shots start coming from ever BOOM, BOOM, BOOM, BOOM, BOOM, BOOM, BOOM, BOOM, BOOM, BOOM, BOOM, BOOM, BOOM, Charlie leaped off the stage to take cover looking for Queen with both guns out. Pull had seen his shit from a mile away.

BOOM, BOOM, BOOM, BOOM, BOOM, BOOM, Charlie's mind was racing a million miles a hours. Seeing all these Mexicans shooting these had to Hundo's people and Charlie knew they all was shooting at him.

"Come on Plane we gone cover you bra".

To the left Pull, Nurge and Kobe was standing there shooting, waving telling Charlie to come there was. Charlie jumped up blasting BOOM, BOOM, BOOM, BOOM, BOOM, BOOM, BOOM, backpedaling the where he Squad was at. King was laying in the middle of the floor dead in a puddle of his own blood hit in the neck and head. Seeing King laying there like that froze Charlie, Kobe garbed Charlie snatching him to safety, in such a daze Charlie didn't even know he was hit in the left leg.

"Where the fuck Queen at Pull?"

"I think she good bra, I saw her going out the door with a few of her folks".

"How you know it was her?"

"I saw her with her momma bra. We got to get the fuck out of here before we all end up in prison bra".

They all ran out the side exit of the building to Pull's Rang Rover, smashing out the parking lot. Every police in the city was turning in the Civic Center FBI, DEA, CPD you name it, they was there.

"I'm hit bra".

"Where Plane?"

"Check on the rest of the Squad Pull".

Queen nor Mrs. Jessie wasn't answering the phone. Squad was good, but King and Roy they both were dead in the shoot out. A total of 17 people got shot including Charlie, 9 of the Mexicans were killed in the mix of the gun fight. Charlie called Queen over and over. They stopped by the house. At Mrs. Jessie's house it was empty. Charlie was starting to go crazy. Jose called Charlie.

"Grandson?"

"Have you heard from Queen or Ma?"

"Torraz got them".

"Who the fuck is that?"

"He said, you had something to do with his son getting killed".

"Who the fuck is his son? I'm lost".

"Hundo".

"He said, you owe him 10 million dollars or they are both are dead. You got 48 hours".

"Dam this some fuck shit".

The Georgia and S.C. rest stop, he said you have to come yourself.

"Just tell him I don't want to hurt them, man".

Chapter 20 Going To Las Vegas Nevada

Charlie had tears rolling down his face when he got off the phone with Jose. It had been a long time since Charlie cried, but today was one of them days. Charlie couldn't keep his head up trying to explain that some nigga had his wife and mother in law. This shit was all his fault. He felt his family might already be dead and he was on his was walking into a trap. Charlie didn't know what to do. The most important thing of it all was to kill Torraz and whoever else came with him. Jose seem scared on the phone, Charlie felt he really didn't want to get nothing for it but fuck Jose the Rarri Gang was gone handle this.

Pull got the whole Squad together on the South Side at his spot off of Calvin Ave to give the rundown. Kobe stood in the middle of the floor doing all the talking.

"Check this out y'all, this how shit got to go we running out of time all ready. Trick and Hot I need y'all to get on the roof in case they got a sniper you feel me. Black you and Gold post up by the exit way, if this shit turn into a big shoot out make sure them suckers don't get out of there.

Doo Doo, Lil Mike, and C.J. y'all gone pull up behind Airplane and Pull in the Van, that way them mego's gone feel that's the only people with bra. Me Nurge, Cee, Yayo and the rest of us gone blind in with the crowd on feet and like normal folks".

Kobe had put together a half way decent plan. None of us had ever been through know shit like this in our life. This wasn't a movie Belly, Boston George or New Jack city this shit was real life. Jose had sent Charlie a picture of Torraz to make sure he knew what he looked like. Come to find out this Mexican Torraz wasn't know joke, he was number 26 on the Americas most wanted list. The Squad was in passion three hours before the tradeoff. As time ticked, all Charlie could thank about was Queen was dead already. It was fucking him up. Jose called Charlie right before he pulled on to the ramp that took you to the welcome center, were it was going down at.

"Son don't do nothing crazy, I need you. Make the swap and come back safe".

"To tell you the truth Jose I'm not sure what I'm bout to do".

"That's why I gave you the 5 million son, pay the money. It's know need for a war".

"Fuck them folks and that money, if my momma and wife are not there I'm gone kill all them folks real talk".

"Charlie you can kill all them and win the battle, but the war will still be going on because Torraz won't be there. He's smarter than that, you owe me one and I'm asking you to pay the money and get it over with son".

"Fasho".

Charlie hung up the phone with Jose and used his Nextel and chirped the Squad tell them don't shot unless he say so. Pull was lost.

"We not gone kill these niggas Rarri?"

'Not if they don't make up bra".

"You the boss, and this yo family. So however you want to play it I'm behind you thug".

Hot notice two gas tanks on a white Tahoe truck, when Pull turned in the welcome center, the gas cap door popped open. Hot chirped Doo Doo telling him to pull the van in front of the truck so they could get a clear shot. C.J. didn't take his eyes off the truck. It was about 8 Mexicans standing outside two Audi's, Pull parked right next to them. Charlie jumped out the car aggressive as hell.

"Where the Torraz at?"

"He id close by. Where is the money?"

"We not bout to do all this back and forth shit I'm telling you that now. Where the fuck is my family?"

The Mexican that was doing all the talking snapped his finger with a smile on his face, one the other mego's pulled out his phone and called someone. Charlie tapped Pull on the arm telling him to get the money. Pull went to the trunk and got the duffle bags out. Charlie bring the money just in case he didn't have a choice but to pay. As Pull walked around to the driver side of the car with the bags, Queen and Mrs. Jessie came running out the rest area. Pull made them get straight in the van with Doo Doo and pull off.

"I'll tell Lord Torraz you are a man of your word".

"Look up on the roof for a second, you see them, all these people around here are with me".

The head mego looked up to see Trick on the roof holding a 30 OTT 6. The Mexican took off took off his glasses. All of their eyes go big.

"So why are we still alive?"

"I don't need to lose any of my men over this, and my family is ok, that's why. We all came here prepared to die, make sure you tell your boss that. Let him know I'm nothing like Jose I live for war. I'm gone respect this robbery, but won't nothing stop me next time. Oh yeah! the dude in the truck right there tell him to stand down LOL".

Charlie waved his hands telling his Squad to come on, getting back in the car pulling off.

"Lord Torraz, here is the money. May I speak to you for a moment?"

"Have a seat", Torraz said waiving his hand in the direction of a black leather chair.

"The Rarri Gang are a group of black guys like never before. Is the money all there?".

"Yes sir, what I'm trying to tell you is, they had us in a situation where they could of killed us all Lord".

"So why aren't you dead then?".

"He wanted to talk to you. He said he respect you as a man and understand your tactics and reason for the robbery. There is no need for war".

"Why are you telling me this Javnn?"

I really believe Hundo cross them some kind of way. No disrespect. He was wrong for killing your son and taking the load, but I'm telling now he's not the average young man with a gang behind him. The other thing you have in the making that might be the man for the job.

Keep your eyes on him than, maybe I'll check into it.

Kobe respected the judgment Charlie made, but he was pissed off on the low. Kobe wanted to kill all they ass. Charlie felt long as Queen was good that was all that matter.

Chapter 21 Messing With The Molly

The loud had just came in. This was Pull first time seeing what Charlie had going on with the gas. Charlie took Pull with him to Oregon, he didn't feel comfortable around Ox by his self knowing what he did to Amari. Pull couldn't believe his own eyes when he saw the set up.

"Plane that's not no gas Rarri, that's that pressure bra".

Charlie and Ox both bust out laughing. This time the weed had double up. Ox had took Charlie's advice and grew like 15 more different kinds. Charlie knew Ox was a real smoker like him, he explain to him that you can have A1 weed but when you got the same shit for so long you will burn a person out on it. Charlie was already ready for the package to drop, he had spots all over the city. Pull had all his young Rarri's ready to work. From the East Side all the way Uptown. This Rarri Gang shit had got bigger than ever. If you wasn't Rarri you wasn't talking about nothing. They drop the prices on the weed, the going rate was 450$ for a zip the Rarri Gang had them for 325$, that was 5,200$

off a bag. Everybody was eating like a fool fucking with the Squad. Pull had a spot in the Dub on 10th street on top of the hill rolling. It wasn't nothing for him to get off a 100 pound bell of mid, 50 pack of loud and a couple of bricks.

The difference of Pull and Charlie was, Charlie let the money do the talking for him. Pull made sure you knew they was running the city. You fucked up 40 or 50 dollars of Pull's money you could believe somebody was coming to see bout yo ass ASAP. Rarri wasn't playing bout his. Jose told Charlie it was time to expand his hustle. 15 million in this city in a 6 year run was a blessing that Charlie didn't have natural life in the feds all the work he was getting in. Queen was down for the change of environment, she been felt we out grew Columbus a long time ago. It only took Queen two months to find their dream home. And looking at that mufucker it was a dream come true.

Las Vegas Nevada was a nice ass city. Queen had trick Charlie like they was going up there to gamble. Charlie took 250,000$ with him just to play black jack. Charlie and Pull had been trying to get to a casino up there so bad.

You know what they say about Vegas, what happens in Vegas stays in Vegas. Kobe swear it wouldn't be nothing better than staying in a sweet Mike Tyson or Big Meeh stayed in. Or even fucking a female M.J. or Puff Daddy had fucked before. The drive was 13 hours long from the C-Town. Charlie slept the whole ride.

"Wake up bae, we here".

"This not the hotel love bug, where are we?"

We at home stank.

What.

Now Charlie understood why Kobe and Lil Marc was with them. Charlie whipped his eyes and looked back to see a big ass smile on Kobe's face. Charlie could see a long ass drive way that was gated off. Right beside the car in the middle of the yard was a water fountain that was made out of a big ass RG, the water was flowing all through it. Queen gave everybody a tour of the house after they got out the car. 7 bed rooms, 5 full bath rooms, living room, dining room, game room, theater, and a inside pool. Lil Marc was so happy.

"Daddy this our new house?", asked lil' man.

Hell yea son, this a long way from Down Town ain't man.

Dad I love you man, I don't never want to go back Down Town.

I know that's right Lil Charlie. {Kobe}

Can this be my room uncle Kobe.

You got to ask yo momma lil nigga.

Please ma, can I get this one please.

Yes Ja'Marcus.

In almost 7 years that was the first time Charlie heard Lil Marc call Queen ma. It was even a shock to her that he said it. Charlie didn't care how much the house cost, his family was happy. But knowing Queen and look at the crib, Charlie knew that bitch cost a arm and a leg. Kobe picked the room next to Lil Marc's bed room and said we wasn't going back to Columbus either.

With75,000$ down sitting at the black jack table Charlie's mind was else where.

With 20 points in his hand only thing Charlie was thinking about the 20,000$ he had bet. Charlie could feel Kobe kicking him under the table. Charlie wasn't paying attention to his ass. Kobe hit Charlie real hard the next time and pointed across the table at a Mexican. Charlie knew the mego from some where. When they locked eyes Charlie could tell something wasn't right. Charlie reached on his side clicking his nine of safety. Kobe leaned over in Charlie's ear and told him {that's buddy from the kidnapping Rarri, get right} Charlie stood up instantly.

"There's no need for all that Mr. Airplane".

"You sure about that folk".

"Positive, we've met before, my name is Javnn, I work for Lord Torraz he wants to meet up with you later on tonight".

"About what?"

"Y'all can discuss that, my job is to make sure your there".

Vegas had a big UFC fight going on tonight. It was flashing everywhere inside the casino. Javnn gave Charlie two front row seat tickets, row 1, chair 6 and 7.

"Tell him I'll be there".

"Fight starts at 9:00".

Charlie couldn't understand what the hell Torraz wanted with him. He hope it wasn't about no meth cause, he was done with that shit. The fight was jam packed. You couldn't hear your partner in there it was so loud. These folks was turnt up bad. Charlie made it there after 10. Charlie took a seat next to a lil ass Mexican, with a Z cut in his face.

"Airplane Charlie what do you know about ultimate fighting?"

"I know a lil bit, the black dude name is Rampage. The white boy name is Ice Man".

"Who do you like?"

"I'll put my money on the white boy".

"Over Rampage?"

"Yeah that cracker go hard".

(laughing) *You know a lil something Airplane. I got 500,000$ on Ice Man myself"*.

"I don't like him that much, to put a half a million on him".

"Airplane what do you know about x's?"

"What pills?"

"Yes".

"A lot, I use to take them from time to time".

"What if I told you I could give you the purest form of it".

"I'm listening".

"Methylenedioxyamphetamine, we call it Molly. I can make you the number one distributor in the whole United States. The way cocaine took over the streets in the 80's, this will do the same thing in the 2000's I'm sure of this".

"Why me Lord Torraz?.

"Jose and myself tried to stay in the bloodline, that you all have created together, but it failed because he wants to be the man, and he wasn't loyal. King was my grandson. The bond between him and Ox will not work because Jose has more than Ox , too much jealousy".

"Only way I can be a part of this is if this stays between us. I'm not sure what happen between you and Jose, but he's been nothing but good to me. If you want to get some money, it got to be like this".

"I can respect your wishes".

Two days later Cook flew Charlie to Oklahoma City to meet MoBee one of Torraz workers, where they was making the molly, 10 bands a key, how could you lose. This shit looked like straight drop crack with a pink tent to it. Charlie bought 20 keys, he didn't want a front yet, he had to see how the shit was gone go first. Charlie and Kobe took a piece small as a nick rock, and was geeked up bad all night. Charlie dam near fucked Queen to death on that shit.

Chapter 22 Money In The Wall

Las Vegas was a wonderful place to live. At night Vegas was amazing, it was always something to do. This was a town that never slept. Now once you get out the Down Town area, you was in a whole another world. The murder rate was sky high. This place stayed on First 48. The MOB and Vice Lords ran the city. For a person like Kobe, this was the land of opportunity.

It was no secret in the streets, talk all over town was Charlie was getting money. He was the spokes peson for the entire Rarri Gang. When he road up and downtown Columbus in a Maybach Landaulet with the roof down it was a beautiful panoramic view. Pull turned in the Flue Tech riding in a Black F-150 trimmed in gold. The 28 inch rims was 18k gold. Pull met Charlie there at the gas station to give him the 800,000$ he owed him. Vegas had Charlie living the life. In the hood, you know when a nigga start getting real money they start riding in the back of they own shit.

The lil chick Kobe had met name Tamber had calmed him all the way down. Shawty was a hood chick, who knew Vegas inside out. Vegas was a real pill popping city. Kobe turned Tamber lil' crew out on the Molly. They were already on the beans heavy. In a very short time they had everybody in the city on the Molly. Introducing Kobe to all the X dealers, he had all them niggas getting the Molly from them 800$ a zip. The whole city was on the Molly fast. To keep Jose from finding out what he had going on, Charlie didn't send none of the Molly to Fla. Or G.A. He was only fucking with Ducc other than Kobe. Ducc was way out there in Oakland, Jose didn't know nothing about him.

"Charlie if I had 150 bands, how many of them bricks of Molly can I get".

"They 11 racks a piece for you bra. I don't care how many of them you get. You must got a play or something".

"Nah bra, I'm just bout to put my foot down out here with this shit".

"Cool Rarri, we came here to chill, just keep doing what you doing".

"Nah, you came here to chill bra. You can get out this shit if you want to, I can't. You got three cities looked down. Dump the work on me Plane, I'm gone hold this shit down out here".

Kobe had put a lot of work in for the team, and never asked any questions. Charlie had to give Kobe a shot. All the shit Kobe had done when the folks got him, lil bra might never get out. Charlie had to respect him, a nigga who wanted to have his own money when the shit hit the fan. Kobe was all in, Charlie had no choice but to back him up.

Cook flew out to Vegas with 300 pounds of mid and 30 keys of cocaine, to put on of the 10 keys of Molly Kobe was getting. Jose and Ox couldn't keep enough weed, Charlie was getting off 10,000 pounds, every other season. It was a whole other ball game with Jose. He had plugged in with the Sinaloa Cartel, dealing with JoaquIn Guzman Loera (aka) El Chapo his self.

Nevada hadn't seen a nigga like Kobe in his time. Kobe had went home and got a couple of this home boys to come back. Cee, Black Da Savage, and Yay, that meant it was four of them young niggas round here that didn't give a fuck.

Those niggas took over the South Side of Vegas , the same as they had back home on the South Side of Columbus. The Vice Lords was deep on the South, while Kobe got some money the rest of the Squad got on the bullshit. Some straight get down or lay down type shit. The Vice Lords didn't even know where this shit was coming from. Cee and them robbing and shooting anyone of the fools that was making a lil noise.

In less than 3 months Kobe had the South on lock, every bit of 50 niggas under him stressing Rarri Gang. MoBee had Family in Kansas, that he was giving Molly to. After his younger brother Flip got busted with 4 keys of Molly, the FBI didn't know what it was. Once the Feds tested the drug in there laboratory, it was name the second most dangerous drug in the US. Kobe plugged in with some of his Rarri's from Atlanta, and the takeoff was real. When Gucci Mane put Molly in one of his songs, he fuck the streets up with it.

Molly had everybody spacing out, especially Kobe. Kobe was rocking like he was untouchable gambling and this fool had shot and killed a Mobb Boss's son in broad day light. He toss a gray bandana on the nigga after he shot him. Torraz was on top of everything, he called Charlie after it happen.

"Airplane I have a lot of love and respect for the Mafia. Do you know one of your men killed a made man".

"I'm not sure what really happen Torraz, but one thing I do know is, he's a made man himself".

"Your friend have to live by the codes, and my people are saying he's not".

"I'm your people. And to be honest the only rule in the streets, is it ain't none".

"They are going to kill him Airplane".

"And I'm gon' kill who ever have something to do with it".

"You got to think smart Airplane".

"I'm not going to think when it comes down to my family".

Charlie called Kobe ASAP and told him to meet him at the house.

Chapter 23 Nasty Ass Hoes; Ain't No Good

Terry was the next upcoming Mob Boss in Vegas. Kobe gunned him down after they got into it at a poker game. Kobe shot Terry with automatic shot gun twice in the chess and once in the head. Yay told Charlie that Terry spit on Kobe, after Kobe bet him out of 15 band. The door man tried to stop Kobe from coming back in the house with the pump, but Kobe shot his ass to in the leg. Yay said Kobe robbed the whole house by his self after he killed Terry.

Turning into Tamber's drive way, Kobe didn't even get time to get the Charger in park before a F-150 pulled up behind him blocking Kobe off. BOOM, BOOM, BOOM, BOOM, BOOM, BOOM, the shooter let over 40 rounds go into the car at Kobe. The shooter left Kobe slumped over the steering wheel. Tamber was in a rampage when she called Charlie, you could still hear the horn blowing as they talked.

"Charlie they just shot Kobe".

"Is he dead sis?"

"I'm not sure bra, they shot over a 100 times".

"Focus sis, go check man".

"He's not dead, but I see blood everywhere, coming from his head bra".

"Do whatever you got to sis get him out the car. I'll meet you at the store up the street, don't let him go to jail man".

Tamber was still flipping out when Charlie and Queen pulled up at the gas station. One of the bullets graze Kobe in the top of the head, two other shots hit him in the left arm. Charlie checked Kobe's pose his self, before putting him in the Range Rover. Charlie couldn't tell where Kobe got hit at in the head, but he didn't see a hole so they rushed him to the hospital. Once the doctors got the bleeding to stop, the police start coming into Kobe's room, the first chance they got they got the fuck up out of there.

"Love you bra, I'm glad you didn't leave me bra".

"Love you to my nigga, you know I wasn't gone leave you up there like dat".

"This shit hurt like fuck Plane. Big bra these niggas done shot bout three of my dreads off". (laughing)

(laughing) *Them shits wasn't growing anyway".*

"Plane these niggas done fucked up bad, I'm bout to show these fools the real meaning of a down South Georgia boy. That's on the Squad".

Terry's uncle Tommy was the leader of the Mob. These was some T.V. gangsters, the type of niggas who would scar you over the phone. Tommy owned a flower shop on 36th Street and Jones. In the back they held poker games. The Squad rushed in the shop and held Tommy's wife, son and another female worker at gun point. Kobe locked the store up so no one could come in behind them. Tommy was shocked to see a group of black men bust in his back room with his family at gun point. It took a man with nuts to pull some shit off like this, Tommy ran Vegas.

"Tommy my main man deal me in".

"Who the fuck are you? I see you have some balls that you don't want".

"I'm Airplane Charlie, or you can call me Charlie Rarri".

"You stupid niggers just sign yo own death papers".

"Tommy you are real disrespectful like Terry. I see now why he's dead. We came here to get a understanding between us. I can tell it's not enough room in this city for two bosses or two Mobs".

Tommy spit across the table right in Charlie's face. Charlie wiped the spit out of his eye and stood up with a smile on his face. The three people that was in the room couldn't do nothing the Rarri Gang was deep in the room with guns out. Charlie grabbed Tommy's wife by the back of her neck, slamming her head on to the card table. Tommy tried to get up, Yay punched him in the mouth sitting him back down. Charlie pulled out his Colt 45 putting the gun to her head blowing her brains out all over the card table {Nooooo} BOOM. Charlie had the devil in him, he grabbed the son next and put his face into the back of his mother's bloody head {So you like spiting on mufuckers.} Kobe put his 9mm to Tommy's head knocking him clean out the chair BOOM.

"What's up with these fools Plane?"

"Fuck them niggas Cee, let them live so somebody can tell the story thug".

The Rarri Gang had the city in a uproar, Charlie showed the whole state of Nevada that his Squad wasn't to be reckoned with. Charlie had to stop going out to hide his face, half the city was reppin Rarri now. He was being spoke of around the town like God or somebody. Kobe didn't slow down one bit, he kept his feet on the gas booming that Molly all over the city.

Shit was starting to get real hot for Charlie in Vegas, so he bought two new houses one in Detroit with a perfect view of Lake Saint Clair and the other one was a stash house that Queen didn't even know about in Denver Colorado. The house in Denver had a safe with money in it the size of two rooms in the projects in B.T.W. The safe was a slick vault behind a wall of a book shelf. Charlie gave Kobe the house in Vegas and got the hell on. Detroit was waiting on the next BMF and in the eyes of Airplane Charlie BMF didn't have shit on the Rarri Gang.

Chapter 24 Vegas Robbers

"Grandson we have a big problem on our hands".

"What kind of problem Jose?"

"The DEA has from a special unit called the Rarri Gang take down. They are saying you group is becoming a uncontrollable Gang across the nations. My source says the DEA label Kobe as the leader Airplane Charlie. Son whatever you do never throw another person out one of those planes again, and make sure you lay low".

"They didn't tell you anything else".

"Yes, a lady name Tanisha King is the head agent over the case, she's from Vegas".

"Fasho Jose, thanks for the heads up".

"We are family Marcus don't ever forget that".

"You know I know pops".

Queen over heard the conversation Charlie and Jose was having. One thing about Queen she was a down ass bitch, niggas don't meet too many females like her in their life time.

"Bae, I wasn't trying to be all in your mouth but I have a idea".

"Talk to me love bug, let me know something".

"If she don't know what you look like, do your research on her like she is doing on y'all and buy the bitch".

"Why I need to know what she look like to buy her bae? I can just make sure she get the money".

"Nah bae, if you pay the hoe you gon' have to keep paying her. Marcus you are a sexy ass man that can have any woman you want. What I'm trying to say is holla at her like you feeling her, make her fall for you then kill the bitch".

"You sure you down with something like that Queen?. What if I got to have sex with her or something?"

"You fucking all these other nasty ass hoes out here anyway. At least it's for a good reason and I know what's going on".

(laughing) *"You hell bae".*

"Nah, I'm real, and I don't want to see nothing happen to you. Fuck that bitch, she trying to take you away from your family".

Queen got online and found pictures of Tanisha. Charlie knew her from somewhere. Queen showed him another picture of her that said she was a black jack player, it all started coming to him. Charlie pulled out his Sprint phone out and scrolled down to the t's and found her name Tanisha King. She was a light brown skinned, little thang, thick ass mufucker with dreads. She was slick and reminded him of Queen a little. Tanisha had a good bluff game with the cards, Charlie wonder what it was like in real life. Soon as Charlie text her she knew exactly who he was. Tanisha let Charlie know that she still wasn't seeing anyone and would love to have lunch with him tomorrow. To Charlie it seem like a walk in the park, but he had to make sure he was careful, just in case she was up on her shit and wasn't trying to pull a flea flicker. Charlie told her to meet at Estiatorio Milos, a nice 5 star restaurant off Northlane Dr. this was a real upscale place that only rich people dine at.

Tanisha made it to the restaurant a few seconds before Charlie. While she was walking through the double doors of the restaurant, Charlie pulled up in his Ferrari 599. She notice the car not knowing it was Charlie. When she realized it was her date getting out as they valet parked his car a smile came across her face. Charlie tip the bell boy a 100$ then walked towards her. The sky blue dress she was wearing fit every curve, this was a bad bitch to be the police. Sitting across the table from Tanisha, Charlie couldn't stop smiling looking at how sexy she was.

"Marcus why are you looking at me like that?".

"I have never seen a woman so gorgeous as you".

"Thank you sweetie. Marcus what do you do, because I have a pretty good job and I can't afford a place like this?"

"My family owns four oil wells, I own 40% of the company".

"Dam must be nice".

"What do you do Mrs. King?"

"I work for the F.B.I, but I really just push a lot of papers".

"You like your job?"

"Somewhat, I like to see people go down that destroy families and life. I like that part".

"Let's talk about us. We should leave work at work baby girl. Let's toast to a great start".

"What makes this a great start darling".

"Cause I can see the future".

"And what does it hold for us Mr?"

"Long vacations and private plane rides all over the world. I could show you a whole new life that your job could ever show you".

"I promise you I wouldn't turn it down either".

Queen told Charlie not to rush the kill and to time it perfect. So that's what he did, for two months straight they went on all kind of dates. Tanisha would get drunk and beg Charlie to come over her house, but Charlie played the role of the perfect gentlemen. Tanisha was falling in love with the devil. She was so comfortable around Charlie, flying her out to LA to see the Lakers and the Clippers play won her over. Chris Paul was her favorite NBA play. Tanisha had been tell Charlie she was always at home working on her case. So when they went to the game, Charlie got Kobe to burn her house down. Before setting the house on fire Kobe broke into the house. And found three boxes full of files on the Rarri Gang. Indictments written up on the whole Squad, even Pull. Over 20 murders, some that didn't even have shit to do with them. She was working with the Columbus Police Department, getting information on Kobe. Kobe took the files with him and set the house on fire.

Charlie and Tanisha both turned their phones off to enjoy the game. As they were leaving out the game, Tanisha cut her phone back on and got the call about her house. Tanisha couldn't understand how in the mix of having a great time, she could lose everything so fast. Not just her home, but case files that would put her on top of her career. She knew it would take 10 years to build another case like that against the Rarri Gang. Charlie called Tanisha trying to make her feel better.

"What's up baby girl, you feeling better?"

"I'm ok, just lost a lot of important stuff".

"Well don't worry about the house, I'll get you another house".

"You would do that for me Marcus?"

"I fuck with you the long way, it's no limits on the things I'll do for you. I told you that".

"Marcus I'm so stressed out. My boss told me he thinks the case I was working on, those guys had something to do with burning my house down".

"There is no telling sweetheart, could be. How about we take a lil vacation?".

"Where? I need it. Plus, I have three weeks of vacation time I can use".

"Anywhere in the world you want to go my love you are worth it, straight up".

"If that's the case, how about the Caribbean Islands?"

"Say no more, I have a few coworkers that I have been promising to take to the Islands as well. Let me get in touch with my pilot real quick and it's a date".

Charlie and Tanisha flew to the game in his small jet. Charlie had been fucking with the Molly and he had bought a G6, big nice ass jet. Tanisha was so into Charlie. They were going to the Islands and she didn't pay any attention to RG in graved everywhere on the plane. It took her almost two hours to ask what it stood for. The way the plane was set up it was broke down into two sections. There were eight seats on both sides of the plane. Charlie stood up and open the door to side B.

"Dam I'm being so rude, let me introduce you to my Squad sweetheart. This is Dirty Redd, that's Yayo, Pull, Hot, Trick, and I know you know who this is".

"Kobe tossed all kind of pictures on the ground he found in her house about them".

"Plane I thought Queen was up here with you, who the fuck is that Rarri". {Yayo}

"Plane.... Airplane Charlie?" {her eyes got big as hell}

"You can stop fucking with that phone baby girl. We out of the country and that shit does not work. (laughing).

"Marcus listen, I love you I can help you. Just tell me what's on your mind".

"Watching you float like a piece of paper is the only thing on my mind".

"Marcus I love you, why would you do this to me?.

"Cause I like to see people go down when they try to destroy my family lives. Yo' ass lucky I didn't kill your son. Kobe feed that bitch to the sharks bra".

{NOOOOOOOOOOOOOO}

Chapter 25 Missing D.E.A

BREAKING NEWS: D.E.A. Agent Tanisha King is missing for 29 days now. Federal agents report her body was found floating in the Caribbean Sea. Sources believe she was tossed out a airplane. There is reason to believe that the notorious Rarri Gang had something to do with Agent King's death.

Charlie was in Vegas for the weekend fucking with his boy TJ. TJ ran one of the biggest underground gambling houses in the city. Straight Texas holding, with a 30 band entry free. All TJ's poker games had a half a million dollar pay off {500,000.} Four tables, ten people at every table. When the first person lost all there chips and tried to leave out the house, 2 niggas burst in the house with guns and mask on their faces. {Everybody on the fuckin ground!!} one of the robbers shot twice in the air. Charlie sat there like they weren't in the room. The short one put the gun in his face.

"*Bitch ass nigga, come up off them rings and all shit you got on*".

"*Listen homie rob them, and just let me sit right here. You must not know who I am, real nigga shit*".

"*You must think I'm going to check yo' I.D. after I blow yo fuckin brains out. Fuck, who are you nigga? I'm going to count to 5...3, 4*".

Buddy slipped when his partner shot the gun again, and he took his eyes off of Charlie for one second. Charlie wrapped his arms up locking it under his own arm so he couldn't get a shot off. Before he knew it Charlie had bone him two times in the eye, dropping buddy down to his knees. TJ pulled the gun out his pocket shooting the other robber in the back. Everybody got up and ran towards the door. Charlie took the gun from buddy and stood over him,

BOOM, BOOM, BOOM, BOOM, BOOM, BOOM, Charlie unloaded the whole clip in his face.

"*Say dog, lets hit these niggas round the way, who be selling that weed*".

"You talking bout in that white house?"

"Hell yeah".

"That's them Rarri Boys, I ain't fucking with them niggas Eddie".

"Man you lame as hell".

"Dumb ass ass nigga they throwing police out airplane and shit, what the fuck you think they going to do to us?".

After Tanisha got killed shit started hitting the fan for the Rarri Gang in Columbus. The police had hit every spot Pulled had, all five of his traps, his mother's house and his baby momma Tasha's house all at the same time. The Feds rounded up over 20 of his lil workers. Pull had caught two sell cases, one on a half a brick of hard and the other one was for ten pounds of loud. Charlie Kobe and Yayo was on South Beach when they got the call. Yayo had just got married. Pull didn't want to go back to prison, he was blaming everything on everybody.

"Plane all that fuck shit Kobe up there doing coming back on Rarri, you need to control that fool".

"What the fuck you talking about pull?"

"The F.B.I. just hit all my spots that's what the fuck I'm talking about".

"This is not the time to start pointing fingers thug".

"Homes be doing the most Rarri straight up. He is the reason we hot like this now, real nigga shit".

"Shit was all good just a week ago my nigga, this shit comes with the game. And to be 100 with you, you doing the most right now".

"Dam you picking that nigga over your own blood?"

"Fuck blood it's about staying free right now. Bra live by the same codes I do, Squad Life or No Life. That's all that counts right now in my eyes Rarri".

"Fasho my nigga".

"Fasho".

Pull was on some other shit, he was too solid to be talking like that. The folks didn't hit know body house but his. This was a lick he had brong on his self that was common sense. Yayo ask Charlie was anything wrong, Charlie said n'all and kept the conversation to his self. Kobe lil crazy ass would of killed Pull ass about some shit like that. Later on that night Charlie told Queen about what had went on with Pull, she told Charlie some real shit. *"Bae I know that's yo boy, but you need to watch him."* It's always the ones you love that you got to watch close. While Charlie was in the bathroom taking a piss, his phone rong. Charlie told Queen to answer the phone for him.

"Hey bra... yeah I'm good, hold on he is right here".

"Squad".

"Boy I'm fucked up down here, I need you to fuck with the struggle".

"Who this is fatty?"

"You got to know that baby boy".

"What's up cuz, why the fuck you ain't been calling me Rarri? What you need me to do get you a green dot, or put the money on yo books. Dam it's good to hear from you".

"Already know it man. I been dealing with this time, really not calling know body. I had to free you, but when I did the judge bucked on my ple".

"What I thought you got 30 do 7 like Pul?".

"Hell nah bra, I got a 30 do 15 but it's all good. They want me to max out".

"Dam I'm slipping I should of knew that shit".

"It's all good Rarri, I just got out the whole the other day, I been locked down for 22 months. Yo momma love me she wrote me a letter the other day and gave me yo number. Last thang I heard you had moved to Vegas and shit".

Who phone you on Rarri?"

"One of my Rarri's, I'm trying to get me one I'm do here in Tailfair State they ain't nothing but 250$".

"I got you bra, I'll text you the green dot numbers in bout a hour. And I'll make sure Queen put some money on your books for you".

"That's the move cuz, you be safe out there".

"Fasho".

Six days later Charlie couldn't believe it then he saw it. "22 year old Ja'Kobe Jackson was apprehended in Rock Hill S.C. after selling two undercover F.B.I. agents four pounds of MDMA also known as Molly with a street value of 140,000$. MR. Jackson is also wanted in Columbus in connection of three murders. Agents are sure Jackson plays a major role in the Rarri Gang organization who are responsible for numerous killing all across the US".

Charlie was sick that his right hand man was locked up. But he knew he had to do something to help him. Trying to put two and two, together it all started coming together slowly but surely. Pull was fuckin with a young niggas projects name Rick, who had some folks up that way.

Charlie remember they rode up there two or three times when the loud came in. That lil town in S.C. they was getting taxed. You could go up there and get off. The nigga Rick had been missing for a couple of days. (Let streets tell it). Pull was hiding deep in Ala., pass Smith station. Shit wasn't adding up right. Queen walked in the bed room and handed Charlie the phone as he set on the bed in a deep thought. But the phone had hung up already.

"Nobody on here Queen".

"It was Kobe, he said he goes to court Monday at 9:00".

Charlie knew he had to flex his muscles for this one. The way Airplane Charlie name held weight in the streets, the lil town wasn't ready for it. The Rarri Gang was about to flip this bitch upside down Monday morning.

Chapter 26 Bodies Flying

Rock Hill Federal court building set directly in the center of a 3way stop sign. The city had two hour parking all around the down town area. Charlie had them young wild niggas from Vegas set in 5 vehicles 3 F-150's a van and a Tahoe. The van set in the front of the building whit eight shooters inside, masked up holding AK-47. Charlie, Yayo, and Dirty Redd, set four car behind the two F-150's to the west of the building. Tamber was the scope girl, if he got free, her job was to make sure he got in the car with her.

It's was about eight F.B.I. agents that walked Kobe outside the courtroom. Once they ways far enough out, to the point they could try to run back and make it in the building John, John floored it. The officers was putting Kobe inside the Suburban when the van smashed into the truck. It was so many News reporters out there, the Police never even seen it coming.

Rarri Dynasty

The Suburban flipped over on to it's side. All eight of them jumped out the car blasting. BOOM, BOOM, BOOM, BOOM, BOOM, BOOM, BOOM, BOOM, BOOM, BOOM, BOOM, BOOM, BOOM. The other three SUV's blocked off the streets. So no one could come in or go out. Art reached in the truck pulling Kobe out the window by the bullet proof vest he was wearing. One of the officers was stuck in the truck with Kobe. He held on to Kobe for a second till Cee point blank range him BOOM. Cee ran with Kobe while they held it down out there in the street. BOOM, BOOM, BOOM, BOOM, BOOM, BOOM, BOOM, BOOM, BOOM, BOOM, BOOM, BOOM, BOOM, BOOM, BOOM, BOOM, they was busting on they ass. The Police couldn't even come out the building and help. All the police in the county start pull up back to back. Kobe made it to one of the F-150's and tried to pull off. All the lil' homies start getting shot, it was looking ugly for the team. They shot the tires out on the F-150, Kobe ran dead into a telephone {BOOM}. Kobe came out that bitch wide open running for his life. Cee jumped out busting, fuck running BOOM, BOOM, BOOM, BOOM, BOOM, BOOM,.

Cee didn't get ten shots off, before they gunned him down. Charlie always knew this was a lose, lose satiation for his Squad, he was just praying Kobe got a ten second window. It was C-4 under all three of the trucks and the van. Tamber was on point, once Kobe was out of sight Charlie push the button and blew all that shit up BOOM!!! The explosion fucked the whole street up. You could see bodies flying 30 feet in the air, all over the steps of the court house. Charlie pulled out like, he was never there.

The Squad was two steps a head the whole time. Tamber got straight on the high way and went to Charlotte N.C. Queen and Cook was already up there waiting on them to fly Kobe out the city. The police put road blocks everywhere but it was too late.

Charlie hit Pull up and told him what they just did, and it would be safer if they all laid low together. Pull was with it, he was ducked off at his sister Amanda's house. Know body didn't know about this house. Pull wouldn't answer the phone nobody but Charlie.

All Pull kept saying on the ride to Baton Rouge Louisiana was "y'all nigga really shoot it out with the Feds, is y'all niggas crazy" Yayo had a lil bitch down that way, she set everything up for us. Yayo was already up on game.

"Where the fuck we at Plane?"

"Didn't you read the sign nigga, we in Louisiana".

"This building look abandon and shit".

"You heard what Gucci said, if you scared go to church".

"Scared, of what? I keep that strap on me. This shit Rarri for real".

Charlie knew there was no half stepping playing with Pull. Pull put one in the head, when Charlie parked in between the two building. Yayo's lil shawty left 3 motorcycles back there waiting on them. All three of them got out the Jaguar and headed towards the bikes. BOOM, was all you heard before looking back to see Pull laying on the ground face down. With his head bust wide open, blood everywhere.

"*Come on Hot*".

Hot was on top of the abandon building laying on Pull with a 30-30. Charlie gave Hot the hand signal to come on. They got on the bikes and hauled ass to the airport, to meet up with everybody else. Cook flew them straight to Harrisburg Pennsylvania, Yayo's girl had some folks up there. It was eating Charlie up to been done did Pull like that. Charlie didn't get to talk to Kobe until it was done already and they was on the plane. Kobe gave Charlie the whole rundown.

"*It was that fuck ass nigga Rick bra.   We had made the play two or three times already*".

So Pull didn't know what was going on.

"*Hell nah, I just knew homes fuck with bra the long way, that's why I was fucking with the nigga. I thought he was Squad*".

"*FUCK MAN!!!*"

"*What's up Rarri, what's going?*"

"Man I done fucked up bra".

"I don't know what you did bra, but it is what it is now, we got to live with it".

Chapter 27 Low Key

The Feds had labeled Kobe the leader of the Rarri Gang after the escape. His face was all over the news stations across the country. The police was saying he had to be Airplane Charlie after the stunt the Squad pulled to break him out. The police found Pull's body and said Kobe had something to do with that as well.

Charlie and Queen branched off to Philadelphia, getting a house in a nice middle class neighborhood trying to blend in. It wasn't long before the Squad went back to their old life. Kobe was back in Vegas in less than seven months. The Rarri Gang was labeled as a terrorist group. In MIA if you got caught with a gray flag it was a automatic five years for gang activity. The police wasn't playing with the Rarri Gang, they was trying to get them niggas off the streets fast. Trying to stay low key Charlie was still bumping into niggas everywhere. From out of know where people start repping Rarri all over the world. As long as the head nigga there had a legit superior that could vouch for him, Charlie was going down there fucking with them niggas the long way.

Rarri Dynasty

All in NYC, Connecticut, Maryland, New Jersey, the Arizona niggas was getting money for real. It was hard to find guns in NYC, Charlie kept them fools strapped up. Before you knew it, Charlie was in the gun trade. All the guns you wanted was floating around GA, try was buying all them mufuckers up, Cook was flying them straight up top.

Time had been ticking like hell, it had been 13 months sense Kobe escaped. Charlie use to watch CNN news every day, this day he saw the most shocking news ever. The Mayors of both city's Columbus GA, and of Rock Hill S.C. had teamed up to bring down the most violent gang they had ever seen. The Mayor of Rock Hill was doing all the talking.

These are the most dangerous group of men I've ever seen in my life. These guys are ruffles and will kill anybody or anyone to get there point across. Even family and friends. The two people most of interest are 23 year old Ja'Kobe Jackson and 25 year old Marcus Smith also known as {Airplane Charlie}. Thank you for all your tips. We are following all leads to bring this entire organization down.

The Mayor was saying they were in deep with over 70 murders. Charlie packed all his shit and went to Michigan, too many people didn't know about his in Detroit. Queen was more worried about Charlie than he about his own self. All she did was cry. Trying to keep a steady mind, Charlie stock up on the Molly and thought about killing both of their asses, Ashely Brown the Mayor of S.C. and James Thomas the Mayor of Columbus. That would be 72 mufuckers he had something to do with getting killed. All the money Charlie had couldn't get him out of this shit. Kobe said he wasn't going back to jail, he was going to make them kill him on sight.

Chapter 28 Hostage

Following the car four todays in a row, today was the perfect opportunity. It was now or never. Ashely pulled into the parking lot of a new coffee shop called Instant Great, with her 8 year old daughter. She was in a BMW. Yay and Trick pulled up on the side of her car, Yay leaped out the car slapping Ashely down to the ground while Jason grabbed her daughter and tossed her in the trunk of the Audi they was riding in. The coffee shop wasn't even open yet, so the park lot was empty. It was a clean get away.

Charlie hadn't been in Columbus in almost five years. But he wanted to be there for this one personally. Mr. Thomas come home to a rude awaking. James's wife did the car pooling for her sons football team. They were going to miss their big game today. It was eight team mates and the mother, trying to rush in the house to prepare for the game when the Squad took them Hostage in their own home. They were scared to death to see five men inside the house with guns, and one dude sitting in James lazy boy chair in a clam manor. They hog tied all nine of them putting duct tape around there eyes and mouth. Seven of the boys in one room and the mother and son in another.

9:32 James came in the house yelling *"honey I'm home"* James almost went in shock when he saw the most wanted man in Georgia sitting in his favorite chair. Savage hit James in the back of the head with the gun from behind, knocking him to the floor. Kobe kicked him in the face two times before Charlie gave them the signal to chill.

"Mr. Thomas sorry we had to meet up like this".

"Where is my family Marcus?"

"They are upstairs".

"What do you want from me? They don't have anything to do with this".

"I see you know a lot about me James. I got one question for you, if you already knew what I was capable of, why would you put your family in harms way like that?"

"I love my family, please don't hurt them".

"I read in a newspaper where you said you won't rest until me and my brother are in jail for the rest of our lives. The crazy thing about it is I don't recall us doing shit to you. So I'm going to give you a reason to hate us. Either we can kill you or go up there and kill everybody up stairs. And I'm going to tell you know it's a lot more people up there than you think it is".

"Fuck nah Plane, this cracker don't get to pick his destiny. I want to give him a reason to take the stand on me. And when he do, the bitch need to be lost for word. I want to hurt him so bad he start smoking crack or sum, real talk".

"Handle it your way than Kobe, I'm just going to fall back".

"Yeah Rarri, sit back, let me handle this".

Kobe went upstairs to the room where all the lil football players were at. All around the room was newspaper clipping of the son and the quarterback. Kobe looked around the room until he found the young quarterback laying on the ground by the bed. Yay and Trick took the boy down the stairs and placed him on top of the counter moving everything out the way. His head was hung over into the sink. Up under the sink Jason found a big ass collared green pot. Kobe filled it up with water and set it on the stove after turning it on. Charlie could tell Kobe was about to do some fuck up shit to the lil' buddy. Yay went around the house cutting all the phone wires.

Waiting for the water to get hot enough, Kobe duct tape James to one of the kitchen chairs so he could watch what was about to happen.

Now you get to be a real witness to the case. You are going to have to live with being the reason this young man never makes it to the NFL. Check that water Savage.

"It's boiling Rarri".

"Be careful and bring it to me Rarr"i.

Savage walked to the sink slowly with the pot of hot ass water. Charlie was stunned about what Kobe was about to do. James tried to jump up, Yay punched him in the back of the head before he could get on his feet good. Kobe poured the water on the boys head slowly. You could see the steam coming off his head as the hot water hit it. The water was so hot the young boy's skin and hair was peeling off his scalp falling into the sink. After all the hot water was out the pot and the boy laid half way in the sink Kobe turned the cold water on him to send the rest of his body into shock. Charlie's stomach was flipping he couldn't take it any more. Charlie walked up and stood over James sitting in the chair.

"Any son of a bitch that will pick his job over his family's life is a pussy ass nigga. That should be yo' ass laying up there dead not lil buddy. Let's see how long it takes for help to come for you".

Charlie pulled out a 357. Revolver and shot James 5 times, BOOM, BOOM, BOOM, BOOM, BOOM, two in one leg and three in the other.

Chapter 29 Most Wanted Man In America

Five days with no food, only two cups of water a day the bitch Ashely was starving. She was duct tape to a chair, getting frustrated, Ashely had flip the chair over and had been laying on her side for days. Charlie left her laying there. Ashely had a bag over her head she couldn't see anything. They only lift it up pass her mouth when it was time to drink water. Her daughter was sitting across the room from her with a chain attach to her left leg. Charlie made sure the lil' girl ate daily. Charlie came in the basement with a glass of water, two slices of bread and a plate full of rice. Ashely almost panicked when Charlie helped lift her up off the ground to sit her straight up. Charlie removed the bag off her head for the first time. She smashed the cold ass rice ASAP.

"Tomorrow is reelection day; Mrs. Brown do you think you wll win"?

"I'm not sure, why are you are doing this?"

Charlie didn't even respond to her. The next time the bag was removed, Ashley was on airplane flying over the G.A. When Ashley realize what was going on she begged for her daughters' life.

"Marcus you have a son of your own, think about him. My daughter has nothing to do with this".

"You sure know a lot about me, I see".

"It's nothing personal I have against you Marcus, I was just doing my job".

"That's how I feel, about this shit business".

Cook drop the latch on the jet. Albany was a small town. Kobe grab the lil girl and pushed her off the plane. Yay didn't waste know time throwing Ashely ass out, right behind her. The police in Albany freaked out. The deaths of the two Mayors made Charlie the number 1 most wanted man in America. The death of Ashely, linked Charlie to all the rest of the airplane killing. The two kids sent the case over board. MP's were out looking for Charlie and Rarri members in Columbus, after President Bush spoke about gangs in our cities.

Shit was hot as hell for Charlie in the streets of Vegas, but he couldn't stay away. Vegas was like home away from home. Kobe had them folks, reppin that Rarri shit heavy all through there. The gang was every bit of 80 to 90 deep in Vegas. They were all young, wild niggas getting money.

Charlie had so many whips, for about 3 weeks he had been slipping through the city, fucking good getting off. Charlie had the work so cheap, it was like he was giving it away. Charlie Yay and Trick was rocking hard. Yayo was in town, Charlie was giving him dam near all the work. Yay turn into the back of the Marriott hotel. Charlie was going to meet Yayo at and pick up the 12 million he owed him. Right before they all got ready to get out of the car Queen called Charlie. Charlie grab Yay by the jacket across the passenger seat and gave him the finger to wait for a second before they got out the car.

"Marcus the folks know what's going on".

"What you mean they know what's going on?"

"The folks done had me all day, they tore the house up, they even know you in Vegas, right now".

"What you told them?"

"What you mean what I told them? They said they been watching Yayo for about six weeks".

"But what did you tell them?"

"You keep talking bout what I told them. I ain't told them shit. But you my baby daddy and I don't know bout all that crazy shit. You need to be asking them so called Rarri niggas what they mufucken said, Not me".

"You act like I'm trying you or something, shit I need to know".

"Nigga you did just try me, fuck you talking about?"

TAP...TAP...TAP...

"Charlie?"

Charlie only heard Yay say his name before he heard the tap on the window. The police walk up to the car. Charlie drop the phone when he locked into the officer eyes. Reaching under his left thigh grabbing for his .45 slowly. Yay rolled down the passenger window down from the driver seat.

"Excuse me gentlemen, didn't mean to startle you. We need everyone to evacuate the property".

"No problem sir, we understand".

Charlie's heart dam near skipped a beat, as Yay backed up and headed out the parking lot. LVPD was everywhere. SWAT was pulling up, that shit was about to get real. Charlie toss both of his phones out the window on the expressway. They didn't know where the hell they were going. They rode for miles. Yayo was all over the 6 a.m News and radio. Money Laundry was squealing about the 12 million dollars. He got caught with some kind of chopper that had 125 rounds bullet in it. Yayo was fucked up. The only good thing they didn't connect him to were killings.

Chapter 30 Pastor Bell

"What's wrong Queen".

"Oh, nothing".

"I'm your mother, I know when something wrong with you. What's going on".

"I feel like it's my fault granddaddy Jose turned Marcus to the monster he is".

"This is the life he always thought he wanted Queen. The goal is now to make sure Ja'Marcus don't follow in the same footsteps. And most of all, be there for him, no matter what, he's your husband".

Charlie couldn't help Yayo even if he wanted too. All the devilish shit Charlie had done - he ran off the only person in the world who really cared about him, Queen. And the only way to get her back was to give his life to God.

Living deep in TX. Charlie and Queen started going to church. The never miss a Sunday. Kobe would go every now and then. The pastor said, *"Come forth let me pray for you, anything asked through the son will be granted by the father"*. The pastor touch him and Charlie got up and walked to the front of the church to pray with the pastor.

"Chief Rivers, Federal Bureau of Investigation; how can I help you?"

"Hey I'm Pastor Bell from Forever Christ Church in Madison Texas. I have some valuable information for you".

"I'm listening", said the captain.

"The airplane killer, I think his name is Marcus Smith".

"You mean Airplane Charlie".

"Yes exactly. I saw him on T.V. last night and I'm sure he is a member of my church".

"Are you positive?"

"Absolutely".

"I will send a team around to check it out in a few hours".

Pastor Bell had been at home looking at gang land, and saw Charlie's picture pop up. The 250,000$ reward is what really caught his eye the F.B.I. had it out for him, but he didn't read the fine print that said you only get the money if the suspect is found guilty in the court of law.

Charlie got up like any other Sunday. Queen wasn't feeling too good so she decided not to go to church. Kobe said he felt like hearing the good word this morning, so it was just them and Lil Marc. Backing out the drive way of the house Kobe realize he had forgot his strap.

"Hold up bra, I forgot that thang".

"We are about to go to church Rarri, we good".

"What thang uncle Kobe?"

"Get out my business all the time Lil Charlie dam". {LOL}

The church was on Vermont St. but there was a detour to Warwick Dr.; so they had to detour all the way around. On West Valley St. one street over from Vermont all you could see was construction workers and three police standing in the road directing traffic.

The red light was broken. It was stuck, flashing red. As Charlie made it to the light a SUV came out of know were hitting the front of the car. The truck hit the car so hard it broke the front axle. Guns was everywhere, even the construction workers had guns running up on the car. All they kept hearing was "DON"T MOVE!! DON'T FUCKIN' MOVE!!" The police slam both of their faces down on the pavement. They took Lil Marc away from the seen fast. They cover up Charlie and Kobe's face and took them to a jail two hours away from the scene. They could not make any phone calls. They locked both of them inside a one man cell.

After sitting in that cold ass cell all night, at 4:31 a.m. a Military helicopter landed on top of the jail to transport them to Guantanamo Bay, A U.S. Naval Station, for federal holding. They shackle them down. Charlie could see the look on Kobe's face and knew he wished he had that pistol with him. This shit didn't have to go down like this, in front of Lil Marc anyway. The MP's cuffed their hands in front of them. Six Military Police walked them both to the helicopter sitting them on opposite side.

"Mr. Airplane Charlie, we have been waiting on you to slip for a couple for months now. I'm gone make your life a living hell".

"Oh really, I guess you one of them super niggas or something".

"I'm the head nigga".

Once the aircraft was air bound for about an hour, the MPs reached over grabbing Charlie by the head.

"We are no longer on American soil, you belong to me now".

With a grin on his face, Charlie head butted him, right in the mouth. Snatching the gun out of his leg strap and started shooting. BOOM, BOOM, BOOM, BOOM, BOOM, BOOM, BOOM. One of the bullets hit the pilot in the back of the head and the helicopter started spinning out of control. It all happen so fast; the other five MP's didn't have time to react. The helicopter swerved left and everybody got stuck up against the door. The plane was going down. Charlie struggled with the door trying to get that bitch open. When he finally got the door to open,

Charlie and three other MP's went flying out the helicopter. Charlie closed his eyes, he knew it was all over so he said his last prayer.

""Lord before I stand in front of your judgment, I want to say sorry for all the pain my reckless ways have caused. Look over my son and don't let him choose me to be a role model. Let him have understanding, and make sure my family know I love them more than life itself. If you can do that for me I'll be grateful. I understand the thing I have done and I'm ready to man up to my punishment. Amen." Charlie opened his eyes to see the helicopter crash, then everything went black.

Chapter 31 No Survivors

BREAKING NEWS:

Helicopter crash transporting two of Columbus most dangerous gang members and drug lords to Guantanamo Bay Prison. The aircraft went down 6 miles away from the prison. 3 bodies were found Slung from the helicopter. After a long sweep of the area all three bodies were Military Police. So far there are no survivors found but the search will continue.

Fatty called Queen soon as he saw the news".

"Queen what the fuck going on?"

"He gon' bra, both of them".

"A plane crash sis? Them crackers done kill my cousin, man. Don't let them folks get away with this shit sis".

"I'm trying to hold on bra and keep my head up. This shit so hard. This shit don't even make sense. They won't tell me nothing".

Dam man, stay strong sis. I'm bout to lay down sis, hit me up if you need.

Fatty set in this cell in a daze, trying to pull his self together. Charlie use to always tell Fatty to save his money, because tomorrow wasn't promise to him. Fatty was blinded by all the weed and green dots Charlie keep him flooded with. But now he understood what he was saying. One thing Charlie use to always say was "look out for Lil Marc if anything ever happen to him, teach him the game. Don't let the streets raise him." For some reason Fatty just couldn't believe Charlie was dead. Fatty felt that nigga had pulled a Makaveli on the streets.

52 months after the crash

For the first time ever Lil Marc was about to meet his father's best friend, who was his cousin Lil Joel. Joel was more like a uncle to Lil Marc than a cousin. Joel had been locked up every sense Lil Marc was born, 14 years and 5 months off a 15 year bid.

Lil Marc had grew up in Detroit for the past five years almost. The people who know Plane was his daddy showed Lil Marc mad respect. Marc was tired of being spoon feed he was ready to jump off the porch and get his own money. Queen drove Lil Marc down to Georgia to see Joel when he got out. When Queen pulled into the yard, the whole yard was thick. Everybody kept saying the same thing when they got out the car.

"*What's up sis?*"

"*What it do lil Charlie*"

"*You look just like that boi Plane, lil nigga*"

Lil Marc knew all these niggas had to be some of his father's good friend. They knew Lil Marc better than he knew his self. Everybody came to the cook out to see Joel. All Lil Marc's real mother family was there to. Charlie's mom Anita was in the house when Lil Marc and Queen walked in the house.

"*Hey granny baby. Looking just like yo daddy*".

"*What's up grandma, how you been?*"

"*I'm ok son. Don't be like yo momma, cause we don't ever see her*".

"Don't do me like that ma. We live all the way in Detroit. This a long ass ride. But you know if you need me I got your back".

"You love your momma -in -law now".

Joel was sitting all the way in the back of the house. That nigga was big as a mufucker. When Joel stood up with no shirt on Lil Marc could see all his tattoo. Fatty was hit up bad everywhere but in the face and hand. He had his legs did and all. The shit reminded Lil Marc of his dad, he was tatted like a fool too. Joel had Rarri Gang Boss across his chess big as fuck, with airplane going through it. Up under the picture it said R.I.P. Charlie. Joel was smoking a fat ass blunt of gas when Lil Marc walked in the room.

"What's up unk? Dam you look just like my daddy".

(laughing) *"Oh yeah! What you got going on lil nigga?".*

"I'm just trying to get my feet wet unk real talk, glade you out, maybe something can shack for me".

"Everything gon' work out. We got to get in touch with yo' granddaddy Jose first".

"I don't know how, ma don't be fucking with him like that. I can't tell you the last time I seen pop's".

"It's all good, you smoke lil nigga".

"Hell yeah".

"Come on lets go on the back, I'll smoke this lil blunt with you".

"Fasho unk".

Lil Marc new his granddaddy was the man, but Queen didn't let him fuck with him like that. The weed was so strong Marc hit the blunt two times and started coughing-like hell, snot and shit running all out his noise. Joel took the blunt back from him ASAP.

"Give me my shit before you get us caught lil nigga. You must smoke that bullshit".

Chapter 32 Ja'Marcus

"Sis, you might as well let nephew stay. It's the summer time he don't got to go back to school yet".

"Ja'Marcus think he grown Fatty, I got to watch this mufucker here".

"I can handle him".

"I already knew this was coming.   His daddy wouldn't let him stay down here, but I'm gon' let him".

"Thank you ma. I'm gon' be straight down here. I ain't gon' get in no trouble".

"You better not, Fatty you better take care of my baby boy".

It took everything for Queen to let Lil Marc stay. She knew his little bad ass was ready to get away and see what the streets had to offer. Charlie had spoiled the hell out of Lil Marc, all the money his daddy had, at 15 he felt he post to be riding in a Porsche something like that. Queen wasn't straight as everybody thought she was. It was 1.3 million dollars in the house that morning when the Feds got him. She still to this day didn't know where the rest of all Charlie's money was at. After moving back to Detroit and opening 3 nail shops. It was like she worked for all the money she had. Lil Marc was ready to get his own money. 3,400$ a week was straight but Lil Marc wanted to see them racks.

Joel was getting it out the mud, 8:00 had to be in the house doe. His parole officer wasn't playing with him. Joel got a house on 6st right across the street from the projects {B.T.W.} and started working out that bitch in the day time. So at night time Lil Marc would be down town with his cousin Ray Ray, trying to sever. Joel had his spot pumping in no time. With them two lil' niggas in there all night with that glass, they couldn't do nothing but get some money. Joel would always tell Lil' Marc "*yo' daddy them, fucked the hood up with that wipe because they had a lot of it. But watch how this drop do and we ain't got nun but a lil of at.*" Joel would leave about a half of drop in the spot every night, Lil' Marc and Ray Ray was getting off. They wasn't fucking up there money so Joel was letting them make it. They were helping him come up.

Ray Ray was Pull's lil' brother. His lil' young ass was deep in the dope game already. When Joel would leave the spot, he would show Marc everything. From dimes to dubs, everything you can name about weed. Joel was buying about 5 pounds of mid. Marc caught on fast. He started cashing out, with his uncle. Marc would buy a zip, Joel would give him one. Dropping 28 grams and getting back, 25 maybe 26. The dope was that man. The spot was doing every bit of 4,500$ a night. Ray Ray use to keep some lil freaks at the spot, watching them get to the money. Marc was loving it.

All in Detroit Marc knew his dad was a made man. The Rarri Gang was everywhere, but Down Town Airplane was a legend. Pull and Kobe was some hell of a niggas in their prime to. For some reason Ray Ray didn't have the same love and respect for Charlie that everyone else did. Ray Ray use to always be saying slick shit but Marc use to overlook it most of the time. Today he just couldn't, Marc felt Ray Ray was trying to show up in front of Teddy P.

"I'm Rarri for real Tedd, these niggas be flexing out here with that Rarri shit. I know what's going on, I don't even got that nigga Airplane name on me. Fuck that nigga". {Ray Ray}

"What you mean, fuck that nigga? You tripping hard now my nigga". {Marc}

"Yeah, you tripping bra". {Teddy P}

"Nigga I ain't tripping, lame ass nigga killed my brother.

Fuck that nigga". {Ray Ray}

Pull got caught with a lot of shit. About 10 million dollars, worth of shit. Like I be telling you bra ain't no telling what happen. {Teddy P}

"Man fuck that nigga". {Ray Ray}

"Look cuz I didn't know my daddy had nothing to do with Pull getting killed. I understand how you feel but you ain't about to just keep saying fuck my daddy like that". {Marc}

"Nigga fuck you and yo daddy". {Ray Ray}

Joel had just walked in the spot as the conversation started getting serious. Soon as Ray Ray got daddy out his mouth Marc took off on him. Marc hit him right in the mouth "BOOM". The right fucked him up but the left dropped Ray Ray down one knee. Marc was on his ass, soon he hit the ground Marc kneed him in the noise. Holding Ray Ray by the shirt the next knee Marc was gone make him black out. Fatty stopped it. Marc had been kick boxing sense he was eight years old. If you was his age, yo ass was gone have to know some. Joel snapped on both of them.

"Y'all niggas tripping. Neither one of y'all know what the fuck happen".

"Well you need to tell us than". {Marc}

Pull was talking crazy Plane said one day. Then the next thing you know Kobe get knocked off. Pull didn't tell him the folks had found all the shit. 6 keys in the apartments on Head street, 100 pounds and 320,000$ cash in his house. Plane thought that nigga had set up Kobe but it was the nigga Rick the whole time.

Them niggas was playing with some real money nephew. Yo daddy told me some times shit happen so fast, you couldn't take it back if you wanted to. Them niggas was living by a whole nother code for real, for real.

Joel cleared all the rumors up that was floating around that Plane killed Pull over the plug, that Plane did it over a couple million dollars, this and that and that and this. Ray Ray still wasn't respecting that shit, he still didn't have no love for the nigga. Marc and Ray Ray got even tighter after the lil' fight.

Chapter 33 Cooking

Marc was feeling his lil vacation. Back in Detroit Marc only had fucked two or three girl in his life. Fucking with Ray Ray, Marc was already about ten strong in Georgia in a month. Today was Marc's birthday. Joel told Marc he was going to give him something he could use the rest of his life. Joel told Marc to come in to the kitchen with him. Joel started getting all his tools out he used to cook his dope up with. Marc had seen him cook a couple of times.

"Check this out nephew; I'm goning to walk you through this a few times than you are on your own".

"That's what's up unk".

"This is a half pot four ounces and shit, this big one is four or more better but you got to do this over the stove. You ain't ready for all that yet. We are going to fuck with the zip pot first. You gon' be able to see the dope good in there. And it ain't too much. You know what a zip of powder weigh nephew?".

"Yeah 28 grams".

"Depending on how much dope you drop, you got to put half of that much baking soda on it., before you put it in the water".

Joel put a plate on top of the Pyrex before putting it in the microwave, turning it on 6 min. In bout 5 ½ min Joel took the pot out. Removing the plate leaning towards Marc.

"Make sure your water is clear. If that shit still cloudy it ain't ready yet".

Joel took some dishwashing liquid, and put a dab of it on the sink. Rubbing the tip of the fork in it. Then sliding the tip of the fork across the top of the water where the dope was at. Next Joel poured all the trash or cut off the dope, until it was just a lil' glob of gel floating around in the pot. After that Joel slowly poured cold water on the dope as it set all the way across the bottom of the pot.

"With that drop nephew you don't even have to fork it".

When the pot was full to the top with cold water, Joel put two ice cubes in it and let it sit for about five min. He swish his hand around in the pot like a tornado until the dope floated to the top.

It took Marc about three good tries to get it right. Then it was nothing for him to drop a two way. Joel had a half a brick that they were playing around with.

"Long as you know how to cook nephew, you can never go broke. Keep saving up yo money, it's gone pay off at the end".

"Fasho unk. I'm gone hold on to mine".

"You ever been to a strip club nephew?"

"Hell nah".

"Put some clothes on. I'm going to let you fuck with me tonight".

Joel bucked on his parole officer to show his nephew a good time. Joel was giving the streets hell (only been out 2 months). His white on white 87 Cutlass T-Top with the 26inch rims on it was one of the cleanest cars in the city. Everybody respected Joel's rank in the Rarri Gang, but they respected him more because he was running up a check and getting it out the mud. Nobody wasn't giving him shit.

The Foxy Lady was the spot to be on Monday nights. The entire club was fucking with Joel from the D.J., to the strippers. Some of these so called big name dope boy were breaking their neck to speak to Joel.

"See the problem with a lot of these niggas in here nephew is everybody want to be the weight man. Fuck all that quick flipping shit, we are goning to keep selling brake down, buying weight running circles around all these niggas".

Drunk as a fool Marc was still trying to suck all the game up he could. Marc was so fucked up Joel and Ray Ray left him in the back of the club. They were by the stage fucking with the hoes. Marc had his head down on the table when the stripper walked up on him.

"They say today is your R-day {Rarri Day}"

"Hell yeah, what yo name is?"

"Everybody call me Sweet Tea. Your uncle Fatty told me to fuck with you".

"Oh yeah?".

From where Marc was sitting, you couldn't see anything. Tea help buckled Marc's pants putting the rubber on for him. The way she was sitting on him look like she wasn't doing nothing but giving him a lap dance. But Marc was all inside her ass. The lil nigga dick was pretty big so Tea was enjoying it just as much as he was. She ended up riding him for about three good songs before he busted. Joel gave her an extra 50$ to take Marc home with her. She would have done it for free, but for the 50$ she freaked his lil' ass out all night.

Chapter 34 Get In Where You Fit In

Ring, Ring, Ring,

Marc just went to sleep a couple of hours ago, his phone was blowing up. Rolling over to see who in the hell kept calling him. Looking at the phone he had eight missed call. Then the phone rang again it was Queen.

"Hello, What's up Ma?"

"I been trying to call you sinse yesterday son. Happy birthday".

"Thanks ma. What you doing?"

"Oh nothing, I'm in Columbus, at yo grand momma house. We gone leave this weekend, your granddaddy Jose said he got you a car. We just got to go get it".

"That's what's up?"

Marc was ready to go anyway, he wanted to see his granddaddy Jose anyway. Joel had already gave Marc the rundown on Jose. Marc didn't know before he came to Columbus that Jose was the plug. With 6,000$ saved up Marc was about to try and get in where he fit in. When it was time to go and Queen seen Marc she all most lost her mind.

"Ja'Marcus I know yo ain't going to try me that?"

Marc pulled his pants up on him. He just knew that was what she was talking about. Queen hated to see Marc sagging like that.

"My bad ma".

"Man I know you didn't put no gold in yo fucking mouth".

"They some pull outs ma. Unk bought them for me, for my birthday".

Queen started checking Marc out good and notice he had gotten two tattoo's one on this neck that said her name. {Queen} The other one was on his fore arms. {Rarri} on the right {Gang} on the left.

"They were letting you do whatever the fuck you wanted to do down here. Go get yo shit so we can go".

"Ma I got yo' name too".

"I don't give a fuck, you shouldn't have got none of that shit. You ain't in no dam Rarri Gang. Go get yo fucking shit so we can go boy".

Queen was mad as a mufucker. The whole ride to Texas she didn't say a word to Marc. It was a long ride from Columbus to Dallas. Queen woke Marc up when they pulled up in Jose's drive way. Marc knew Jose had money but not like this. The first car he saw in the drive way was a big boy 760 BMW, that was Marc's dream car. Jose walked out the door as Queen pulled up to the house.

"My favorite grandson".

"He's your only grandson, granddaddy".

"That's why he's my favorite. I don't know why you don't let him come around more often Queen. How you like you truck Ja'Marcus".

"You talking about that gray one right there?"

"Yep, that's all you son. Black leather seat, 6 dis CD changer, 22inch rims, that's how y'all young guys like it now a day's right".

"Like it, I love it pops".

"Come inside, talk to me for a lil min, it's been a long time sense I seen you. How school going for you. By the way happy birthday".

Marc didn't know Jose had it like this. Joel use to always say if we get under Jose, that nigga would change our life. Jose and Marc played a few games of pool talking about school and shit. Jose told Marc straight up that Queen didn't want him to be a part of his life, because the effect that took place with his father. Jose told Marc that he had to respect that, because Queen was a good woman trying to raise him right. Queen was tired of hearing all the bullshit Jose was talking, so she went and laid down because she knew she had a long drive in the morning.

"Grandson, can I talk to you like a man for a second?"

"I wouldn't want it any other way".

"You remind me so much of your father. What do you really know about your mother?"

"I know she mean well by me. But I'm getting to old for all that lil' kid shit, she think I am suppose to be on."

"I can respect that, but I was talking about your real mother".

"Oh! She got killed when I was young. I don't even remember her like that. My uncle Fatty said my dad was into all kind of shit back then, anybody could of did that shit to her. But check this out, I need to talk to you about some while I got the chance".

"I'm listening so talk to me".

"I got almost 6,000$ pops I'm trying to get me some dope".

"What cocaine?"

Yeah, I know how to cook my own doe and everything.

I'm not sure if your ready for all that yet. The first time let's try it out with some Marijuana, and see how you do with that then we will go from there. You can keep you money, it's bad enough you have to ride all the way back home with it.

Fasho pops, but why you ask me about my momma for.

"Yo father was a great man if you got to know him loyal as they come. One hell of a business partner. But he was sleeping with the enemy son".

"What you mean by that?"

"Your mom killed your mother son. I'm not trying to brain wash you, but I felt that was something you needed to know. She makes me out to be the bad guy but we all have secrets in our closets".

Chapter 35 Fucking With Nala

Jose gave Marc 25 pounds of mid on the strength. Queen let Marc drive his own truck back sense he had a permit. The 25 bags of mid that was in the truck, wasn't nothing compared to tell news he had just heard. That shit made Marc start looking at his daddy differently. All that gangsta shit he did in his life, Charlie post to have tossed her ass out one of them planes.

Marc had his mind made up time they made it home. All that bullshit bout come in the house at 12 and all that, that shit was over with. Marc couldn't respect that shit. It wasn't the fact she killed her, but the point she never told him. Anything can be explainable, if you explain.

When Yay got hot back in the day, Charlie made sure he was straight. Yay had twins by Kia, Nala and Nick. Nick and Marc grew up together for the past 6 years on and off. Kia still lived in the same house Charlie bought her almost 7 years ago. Marc was wore out from the drive, he couldn't wait to get up and go fuck with Nick.

Marc had never seen this much weed in his life. Jose put the weed in the back of the truck the BMW X3 was so player, he knew Marc wouldn't have any problems getting back. Marc grabbed a couple of pounds out the bag, put the rest of it up, and headed over Nicks house. Nick called Marc while he was on the way already.

"What's up baby boi? You still in Georgia fool?"

"Nah, I'm back bra. You must didn't get that picture massage I sent you bra".

"Yeah, I got it. Who does the truck belong to? That bitch is clean".

"It's mine. My granddaddy got it for me".

"You got to come fuck with me".

"You already know it. I'm on the way".

It took Marc every bit of 25 min to get to the West Side Detroit. Nala was sitting on the porch when Marc pulled up. Nala and Nick was 17, Nala was a bad lil red bone. Kind of skinny, but had a nice body. Young gold digger, she was trying to see who was up in that truck.

"Oh what's up Marc I didn't know that was you".

"What's going on Nala, where your brother at?"

"He in there, dam I see you got some gold in your mouth".

"Yeah, my uncle fucked with me while I was down there".

"You got some tattoo and everything. You grown now huh.?"

"I see you got yo eyes on me".

"Boy stop, yo' young ass would know what to do with a bitch like me if I gave you a chance".

"Give me one and see then".

"Keep playing I just might".

Marc got out the truck smiling and walked in the house. Kia was sitting in the living room when he walked through the door.

"Hey Mrs. Nala".

"Hey Lil Airplane, how was your trip?"

"It was cool, got to see all my folks".

"Fatty got out didn't he".

"Yeah he got out, he super big too".

"I bet he is 15 years hell. Well I'm glad you had fun. Happy late birthday. Nick out there in that back yard".

"Fasho, thank you to Mrs. Nala".

Nick was in the back yard with his home boy DJ playing 21. The rim on the goal was bent and they didn't have any nets on that bitch. This shit was hood for real. Nala came and stood on the back porch while Marc watched them play ball for a min. Nala stood there looking sexy as ever. Being bow legged gave her a stand that any nigga couldn't resist. Marc knew who DJ was but they wasn't cool like that. But DJ and Nick was tight, plus DJ was Rarri, so Marc didn't mind fucking with him when he came around.

"Dam bra y'all back here getting all stank and shit, you ain't about to get in my car like that".

"That's what's up, I'm gone fuck with you in a second DJ, let me see what this fool talking bout".

"Bra good he can ride, we just finna been a couple of corners".

"I want to go to then". {Nala}

"How about when we come back, me and you get together on some solo shit".

"Whatever. I hear you".

"Sis get yo lil gold digging ass on somewhere. Don't let that cuteness fool you Rarri she money hungry bra".

"Get yo lame ass on somewhere Nick, with yo lil broke ass. I got a job, I get my own money I don't need no nigga. Fuck wrong with you".

All three of them got in the truck. Marc went in his pocket pulling out a pack of Newport shorts in a box, then felt in his other pocket while he was driving and pulled out about a half OZ of mid handing it to Nick sitting in the passenger seat. It was some good weed, nothing like the shit that was floating Detroit. All the mid in the city was brown with a hundred seeds in it.

"This that Georgia bud right here DJ, this shit round here ain't talking bout nun".

"Yeah, that weed right there look straight".

"This all you brought back Marc?"

Marc pulled over into the KFC parking lot, reaching in the back seat getting the Jordan book bag that was sitting next to DJ the whole time. It was three pounds of mid inside the bag. Marc pulled 6 half a pound bags out of the book bag laying it on his lap.

"I am going to try and get me some money, I don't know about y'all niggas. My granddaddy own boy. I'm talking bout like a mufucker".

"Bra real Rarri shit I'm with it".

"Me to my nigga, I'm ready to get me some money too".

"I got the money and everything, we can get us a lil' trap. *Just us three we ain't fucking with all these niggas. I don't care if they Rarri or not".*

"Fasho".

"I know that's right".

Marc gave Nick two pounds of the weed and gave DJ the other one. 900 a pound they couldn't beat that ticket. Plus they had the best weed in the city, only thing they could do was come up. Joel showed Marc, long as you take care of your team they gone take good care of you. Only way you gone get some real money, is if everybody in yo circle eating.

Chapter 36 Mama Tripping

Marc had been chilling over Nick's house the last two days. The first day with the weed Nick and DJ did alright, but the second day started off early for them. Nick had jumped almost a half a pound already and it wasn't even 12:00 in the afternoon yet. Marc had been fucking with Nala the strong way. The past two days Marc had been making sure she got back and forth to work. It was about 2:30 in the morning when Nala feel asleep on him, it was late so Marc went home. Queen was standing at the top of the stairs when Marc walked in the house.

"Give me them dam keys to that truck, that's straight. You not about to come in here any time of night".

"This my car, you didn't buy that car".

"I don't give a dam who bought it. You been trying lately every sense you came back. Don't let that shit yo folks been down there telling you get you fucked up lil boy".

"*Telling me like what? You killed my momma? You thought I didn't know that didn't you?*"

Queen's mouth dropped. That was the last thing she thought he would say. She couldn't believe Marcus had told Joel.

"*Oh, you don't have anything to say about that shit do you? It's all good, I figured that*".

With tears coming down her face, "*Ja'Marcus I'll be dam if I let you sit here and disrespect me like this. I been a dam good person to you. If you feel like you know everything and you a grown man there's the door*".

Queen wasn't expecting the reaction she got when she said what she said. Marc went upstairs and packed his shit. The rest of his weed and money was the first thing he grabbed.

It take to much cloths and shoes like that. Marc got right back in the truck and pulled off.

Knock, Knock, Knock,

Kia came to the door half ass sleep.

"Marc I thought you went home?"

"I did my mama tripping. You mine if I stay over here tonight".

Boy you know I love you, come on in. you don't even have to ask know shit like that. Gone back there with Nala, Nick and DJ left right after you did.

Marc didn't even wake Nala up, he just laid on the bed beside her and fell asleep. Nala didn't even know he left in the first place.

Marc woke up to Nick standing over top of him holding a gun. Marc could barely see but he saw that gun in Nick's hand.

"What the fuck you doing bra?"

"I'm trying to see do you want to buy this mufucker. You don't let sis fuck you so good yo ass won't wake up".

"Yeah, I want it, what they want for it?"

"90$, and Blade up the street want to know can we sell him a pound".

"Why you just didn't sell him one of yours?"

"I had to make sure it was some more first, before I sold him all my shit".

Marc got up and went to the closet were he put all his stuff, and pulled out the weed. Nick didn't know Marc had that much weed. Marc gave Nick a bag of the mid to make the play with. It felt great for Marc to wake up to a 900$ play and a brand new gun. Mrs. Jackie, DJ's mom house was the spot. Everybody use to be standing in her yard getting off. Mostly older niggas, DJ was sucking up all them niggas money. That afternoon, DJ reed-up and Marc gave him 3 whole pounds. Sander Ville was really a crack neighborhood. The whole hood sold that bullshit water whip dope. It was hard to find good dope on this side of town. Everybody had the same shit because it wasn't too many cooker.

The same two, three niggas was cooking up everybody dope. In Detroit it was a blessing to know how to cook dope. Georgia wasn't like that everybody felt they had a hell of a wrist down that way. Marc knew what he was gone do time he got his hands on some good clean. Nothing but that drop, that glass was gone roll.

Nala was starting to get beside her self. It was just now starting to crank up, and she wanted a ride back and forth to work every day. Then once she was off she still wanted to go here and there.

I thought I told you I got off at 4 nigga, don't be having me sitting outside.

"Wendy's got a lobby, get yo ass a hamburger and sit down some were. Shit you know I'm coming. You must be scared or something".

"Scared you don't even believe dat, yo got dam self".

Nala was one of them club hopping type of females. Not going home Marc was staying over kia's house, the pass couple days the money had been flowing good on Marc's need. Fucking Nala hadn't even been on his mind. Two nights in a row, without touching her, she was starting to do too much popping. Tonight was the night.

Chapter 37 Prince Charlie

Marc knew the Rarri Gang was big, but it was like he found something new out every day. Marc didn't grow up in Sander Ville like nick did so the streets didn't know Airplane was Marc's daddy. Nala walked in the house were Marc was at playing the game and told him "Nick said *come here real quick baby, I don't know what he wanted.*"

"What's up bra?"

"Man tell these clown ass niggas who your daddy is just by looking at you".

"Plane, you know what's going on bra".

"I still don't believe he Airplane son, straight up".

Marc pulled out his phone without saying anything, calling Ray Ray on speaker phone.

"What's up lil Airplane, what it do cuz?"

"Shit just cooling, on my Squad shit, you got to know dat".

"Already fucking know it".

I was just fucking with you Rarri, I ain't want shit for real.

"Stay focus my nigga you Prince Charlie lil cuz, you got to go hard. I know they reppin that Rarri shit up that way. Get them niggas rocking right, and take that shit over up there like Plane would have did".

The four niggas that was standing on the porch didn't know Marc lil young ass had that kind of pull. The hood thought Marc was just a young green nigga, fucking with Nala. All the attention Marc was getting was cool with him. Six out of 10 the nigga smoke weed, that's going to make him a play for Marc in the long run. Nala wasn't feel all that dick riding them niggas from the hood was doing. Nala had stank lil attitude the whole day. On the way to work Marc got tired of her looking like that.

"What the fuck wrong with you?"

"I don't know why you showed these pussy ass niggas round here yo' hand like that. You better watch them asses".

"Fuck them niggas bae".

"Listen to me Marc them real cut throat niggas. They stress that Rarri shit and Squad shit but them niggas all for them-selves. Trust me I know all these niggas you don't".

Shit like that was the reason Marc fucked with her, shawty was gone keep it real no matter what. Slowly shit started changing for Marc but advancing at the same time. It had been six days sense he been home, or even seen Queen. At the same time Marc had gotten off every bit of 17, 18 of them pounds. That shit with Queen wasn't on his mind no more. He was grown now, in his eyes. Joel called Marc just to see what he had going on.

"What's up nephew? What it look like up there for you?"

"It's rolling up here for me unk".

"I told you young nigga, you can't buy clean from anybody. A nigga gone remix yo ass".

"I ain't even fuck with no dope yet unk. My granddaddy just gave me a couple pound of weed".

"I told you, that nigga on nephew. You think he gone fuck with you?"

"I believe he will unk, real shit. I'm just trying to get off this weed I got".

"This what you got to do; I'm gone let you spend money with him. Once he see you got plays like this he is going to fuck with you".

Marc hit Jose up and found out what was going on. Jose had the type on number, you had to get some money. 300$ a pound of weed, 22.5 for a key of cocaine. The only catch was you had to spend 80 racks or better. The lowest you can spend is 75,000$, but no matter what you spent it's an additional 5,000$ for the delivery fee. Marc told Fatty that the dope was 25,000 a brick. If Joel bought 3 keys like he was saying, it was a lil cap in there for Marc. And at the same time he could get some weed for the low. Joel told Marc to give him two weeks and he would be ready.

Kia was fucking with an old cat from the East Side name N3 who had that work, for a good number. Some A1 clean. Marc knew he had to run up, as much as he could before his uncle got there.

Marc bought 3 zips of soft for 10.5 a piece and got him a lil spot. Each one of the ounces he drop came back like 26.8, some like that. That real glass house. It didn't take know time for the word to get out that Marc them had that drop down there. It was hard to make a dime from 16th Ave on back. N3 started paying Marc to cook his dope. 150$ a OZ you couldn't beat that, and the nigga want you to cook up a nine every time. Every 3, 4 day a free 1,350$. Before you knew it a lot of niggas started letting marc cook they dope. After playing with the work so much Marc thought his self how to stretch. That way them niggas would never be good as his.

Chapter 38 Greyhound Bus

Fatty hit the road five weeks later. Marc had ran up a check by then. Fatty didn't know he was a made type of nigga all around the world. He had never left Georgia. Only time he ever left Columbus was from going from prison to prison. The niggas in the D was ready to meet Joel. The streets felt Airplane was one of the most street's niggas worked this earth, but Marc didn't understand how he let Queen kill his momma. She should have been one of them mufucker who came flying out them planes.

By time Fatty got there Marc had 35,000$ of his own money. Shit was flowing good for him. Marc and Nala had apartment of the South Side of town. Nala wasn't feeling living with her momma and Marc had all that money. Marc even got her a 2002 Cougar, but before you knew it that was Marc car and she was riding around in his truck. Joel didn't know what kind of power he had in the streets. When Joel pulled up at Kia's house, the whole West Side of town was out there to see this nigga. Joel knew he had rank but not like this. It was some niggas reppin that Rarri shit for real.

Who just wanted to meet Fatty. Marc knew shawty blew Joel mind when she told him her son name was Joel. Marc was on the phone with Jose when Joel pulled up.

"Yeah pop. I got the play now, I can send the money to you".

"What you say you need son?"

"50 pounds and 4 keys".

"Let me get in touch with OX and he will tell you what to do. One of us will call you before the night is over".

"Fasho".

When Marc got off the phone with Jose, Joel had everybody in the house sitting down putting them up on game about the Rarri Gang, Joel didn't even know Marc was behind him.

"N'all Rarri, y'all don't never post to beef with the GD's, we fuck with the G's the long way. Being gangsta is something that's just in you like the book say. John Gotti and the MOBB was gangstas. This Rarri shit you got to live it, not just go to war bout. RIGHTEOUS, ANGLES, ROYAL, RUTHLESS, IDOLS.

Righteous is the first word, the last word id idol. My nephew is the defection of Rarri, he want his own money, his own name for his self. Like real niggas do".

Listening to Fatty talk Marc learn a lot of shit about the gang and were he came from. When Joel realize Marc was standing right there he step in the hallway to holla at his nephew. Marc ran Joel down on the conversation he had with Jose. Now he was waiting on them to call back. In a short time he got the call he was expecting.

"Ja'Marcus?"

"Who is this?".

"OX your granddaddy. You don't know my voice boy?"

It's been a long time pop's. What's been good with you?"

"Listen to me carefully, 105,000$ is how much you need to give my people. They will meet you tomorrow at the Gray Hound bus station. Some where around 6:00 and 7:00".

"Everything is going to be on point pop's".

"I trust you son".

DJ been missing for the past 4, 5 day. He was like 200$ short on his last package. Marc wasn't stressing it. Both he and DJ had a bond like him and Nick in his eyes. DJ was standing on his momma porch when Marc pulled up on him. DJ walked to Nick side of the car.

"Dam Rarri you must don't sell dope no more". {Marc}

"It's not like that bra. I'm gone give you that money I own you today when my momma get off". {DJ}

When yo momma get off. {Nick}

Bra we came over here to check on you. Fuck that lil money, if you don't want know money that's on you I'm gone get me some. {Marc}

Bra you know I want some money bra. That pussy ass nigga Slim stole my money the other day. My momma said she was gone look out me today till I get on my feet. {DJ}

"Who the fuck is Slim?" {Marc}

"You know Slim Rarri, the nigga I showed you the other day? The one I said beat dat body?". {Nick}

"The nigga who go with yo sister". {Marc}

"Where that nigga at bra?". {Nick}

"Y'all know homes keep that strap on him". {DJ}

"Me too, and one in the head. You got yo strap on you Rarri". {MARC}

"You got to know that". {Nick}

"Get in bra, we about to pull up on this clown and get that lil money back". {Marc}

Marc and Nick were mad as DJ was. They didn't know who in the hell this fuck nigga Slim thought he was. Marc had already told his self if Slim didn't have that money when they saw him it was going down. They was going up empty riding around looking for the nigga. Nick had a play for a eight ball so Marc shot back to Mrs. Kia's house that's where Nick told them to meet him. DJ notice the blue lil Honda on the side of the road.

"Say Marc he got to be in there with unk, cause that's the car him and my sister been in right there with that paper tag on it bra".

All three of them jumped out the car instantly. Kia was standing on the porch when they got out the car. Mrs. Kia knew something was wrong. She tried to grab Marc but he snatched away from her.

"Ja'Marcus what the hell is going on? You better not put yo hands on my daughter".

Marc pass Nala headed towards the back yard. Slim and three other niggas was standing in the back yard trying to suck up some game from Joel. A fuck nigga trying to get some game from a real nigga. Soon as Marc laid eyes on Slim he pulled his pistol out. And flushed up on him. When Marc got in arm reach of Slim he bowed him in the chest, knocking him over the BBQ grill he was standing in front of. Gun in Slim face as he laid on the ground.

"Fuckin nigga. Where is the money?"

"What money lil homie, what you talking bout?"

"You think I'm playing don't you, bitch ass nigga. I ain't gon' ask you no more".

"I bought that car with it bra man, don't shoot me Rarri".

"Bitch ass nigga, give me those keys, before I pop yo' stupid ass".

"That wasn't even yo' money Marc".

{BOOM}

Marc hit Slim in the right leg with that 9mm. Kia tried to grab the gun after Marc had already shot him.

"Ja'Marcus stop" yelled Joel as he grabbed Kia out the way so she wouldn't get hurt.

Marc kick Slim in the face then stood over him putting the gun to his head.

"If you don't give me those keys folk, I'm my daddy I'm gone kill yo ass back here".

"They are in my back pocket Marc. The title is in the glove box bra. Please don't shoot me no more".

Chapter 39 Deep Shit

The next day at 6:15 the work had landed. Marc took Nick with him to the bus stations to pick up the package. Marc was getting a whole brick and 50 pounds out the dill, the next time he was gone have enough money to make his own move. It was a good thing to have that much work, but Marc already heard DJ sister Cent had told the police what went on. Nala said all she wanted was her car back, Marc wasn't trying to here that shit doe. That bitch wasn't getting shit back.

Marc wasn't stressing none of that fuck shit Cent was on, he was on his way to the spot. Getting all his shit together headed for the door Nala stopped Marc.

"Marc you don't need to take all that shit with you to the spot. You know they saying them folks riding around with a picture of yo ass".

"Man I'm about to go cook my dope up".

"You can cook that shit up here bae, you don't need to go down there period Marc".

For some reason Marc took Nala's advice and stayed home and put the work together right there. Marc called Nick to come to the house and pick up the 6 zips he cooked up for the spot. Marc rented a movie and stayed in the house for the rest of the night.

Marc had so many missed calls when he woke up he was out the door before the cows could crow. Straight to the spot he went. It was a good thing know body was there when Marc got to the spot. It was a Friday to, it was gone roll. Marc looked in the cabinet over the sink where they kept all the work, Nick and DJ had gotten off the whole bomb. Wasn't nothing inside the cabinet but the 5,400$ Marc wanted for the 6 zips. Marc looked out the back door of the spot, he thought he heard something out there but didn't see shit. Marc lite the half of blunt he had behind his ear. Walking towards the living room, before Marc could blow out the first cloud of smoke {BOOM} the front door flew open. "Everybody on the ground DPD" the police came through the front and back door, wide open. Two of the officers wrestled Marc to the ground the rest search the house.

"This is him, Sgt".

"Who else is in the house with you?"

Marc was scared as hell on the low. But he knew it wasn't know drugs in the house so he was gone be ok. While the police tore the house a part the set Marc outside in one of the squad cars. The whole hood was out there watching the spot get busted. It was about 15 min before Nick and Kia made it around the street. Nala and Queen pulled at the same time. Marc could see Nala and Queen talking to the folks. The only thing the police found in the house besides the money was a old rusty ass 10 gage shot gun Marc told DJ don't buy. The officer looked mad as hell when he walked up and opened Marc's car door.

What's your name son? How old are you?.

"Ja'Marcus Smith, I'm 15".

"You lucky, you in some deep shit son you know that? What do you want me to do with all your money, give it to your mom?".

"Yeah, you can give it to her".

Marc might have stayed on the seen 30 more min before the police transported him to the closet RYDC. The police wouldn't let Queen speak to Marc at all. After the police pulled off with Marc, Nala was trying to find out what was going on with her man.

"*Ma Q what they charge Marc with?*"

"*They saying he got a lot of charges. He pose to shot somebody the other day. Plus they found a shot gun in the house when they raided it*".

"*Ma Q., I know that bitch Cent sent them folks down here, cause Marc just left the house*".

"*Well they gave me almost 6,000$ they took off of him. I guess I'm about to go get him out*".

"*And while you go get him out I'm about to go round here and check this hoe Cent, cause she got me fucked up. Messy ass bitch done put my nigga in jail*".

The charges already had bonds set on them when Marc made it to the RYDC. 5,000$ for aggravated assault, 2,500$ for possession of a firearm. Once you put the taxes all on it the bond came up to 8,743$.

Queen was at the jail with the money before Marc could even get dress all the way out. Marc was never so happy to see Queen as he was walking out the jail. Queen didn't say a word while they were riding.

"Thank you for coming to get me".

"You welcome, where you going, I got to go and get my hair wash and set".

"To Mrs. Kia house?"

"You better sit yo ass down somewhere. You can try and be like yo daddy if you want to. But I don't got no 10,000$ to be bonding you out of jail with".

Queen pulled up in the drive way, Marc had a smile on his face.

"Thank you man, I don't need no help doe, I'm good out here".

Nala was sitting on the sofa when Marc walked in the house. You could tell she had been fighting, but Marc didn't ask her or nothing. They just chopped it up with the few people that was in the house and then went home.

Chapter 40 Shot Gun

Marc was getting better and better in the kitchen, so to make up for the lost he took he was going all in. Blizz had a recipe back home that was so nice. Adding goat milk in the dope keeping it hard and solid. They didn't have a stop know more so the pull up game had to be strong. Marc put Blizz recipe on the streets and fuck the blocks up. 30$ grams and they will pull up if you just want one. But still keep glass for the smokers. Riding around in rental cars working, they was getting it in way harder, then in that spot.

After shooting Slim, Marc won all the respect of the streets. Slim was post to be a real nigga, and put the folks in the game. The streets didn't make niggas like they use to. DJ was buying up all the straps he could. Nick was on his flashy shit, Marc was all over the above. In the mix of buying some 22inch rims OX called Marc and told him he was in town. To meet him at the house for dinner so they could talk. Even know Marc wasn't fucking with Queen like that he still was gone go see what OX wanted. He always treated Marc like a son.

"Old school, I see you still got your swag granddaddy".

"Grandson, I came all the way down here to tell you a few things. All the people in your life right now that mean to seem you well really are not. Queen always had your best interest in life. It's a lot of poison around you. Something in life you can't forgive or forget. The best thing to do is move pass it. I bet you didn't know your father killed my son, Queen's father. Queen loves you son, Jose is the devil himself. But this is the job we sign up for, so let's work".

"I respect what you are saying pop".

"Now that's over with, I need a favor grandson".

"Anything pop".

"My people couldn't pay for the whole package, so before I front it to them I'll give it to you".

"How much it is pop? You know I don't mind. I want some money, real nigga shit.

"It's 200 pounds, call me when you get done. Maybe we can keep something going on".

"Fasho".

This was Marc's first time seeing Queen since she got him out of jail. After talking to OX for a while Marc walked in the kitchen to get something to drank. Looking at Marc, Queen could tell he was everything she didn't want him to be. Nice looking jewelry a young dope boy. The bad part was he looked like he was doing pretty dam good. Marc caught Queen off guard when he hugged her from behind.

"I just want you to know I love you ma".

"I love you to son. You always got a place you can call home".

"I already know it".

Ox weed got better and better every drop. Marc didn't tell know body he had all that weed. Marc start fucking with all the niggas in the city that was Rarri giving them the weed for the low. When they ran out of crack Marc still had bags on bags. Marc waited on his uncle fatty before making another move. Buying lil 9's and shit from niggas in the city till Joel was ready, Marc found out who was really getting some money out here. Marc was getting the bricks for 22.5, 1,100$ a zip that was 39,600$ a key. That was a 17,000$ cap. OX gave Marc 200 more pounds of weed along with the 3 keys he bought.

Marc sold all three of his soft and put 2.7 grams of cut on every OZ. {B-12} The dope was so good it didn't even matter. Marc sold all his work and went back and got 4 more keys. Cooked a whole one up half straight drop, and the other good wipe. Marc turn a half a brick in to dam near 26 OZ. The other three just like last time. It took seven months for Marc's court date to pop up. They was talking about 3 years Marc bucked that shit he went on the run.

This wasn't the right to go to jail. Detroit had never seen a young nigga like Marc before. Two Cutlass's one on 28's the other on 30's. The T-top one was on the 28's, cocaine white with the smoke gray top and insides. The 28's was the same color gray racing rims. Queen was a lil mad her she didn't have any pressure on Marc about it. Shit was at the top of the charts for Marc, the streets was calling him lil Airplane. OX told Marc "You know how to get some money just like your daddy, now let's see what you gone do with it."

Marc and Nala had been beefing the last couple of days. Facebook was making her believe that Marc was fuck Star, her first cousin. The shit was some bullshit doe. Star was a fine ass lil stripper bitch. But it wasn't anything like that, she like to smoke weed and talk big shit. Nick and his old lady was into it as well so him and Marc was staying at the motel room. Bouncing from room to room, Marc had fucked a lil freak in a room earlier that morning at the motel 6. So Marc and Nick went back there for the night. The police was riding through slowly.   They were doing spending people tax money doing nothing. Marc had just bought an automatic shot gun for 3 grams. They had that in the car to. That bitch was so fire Marc had to buy it. It was sawed off, with a shoulder strap. It fitted right under the Lion's coat Marc had on. You couldn't see it at all. But it wasn't hard to get to.

Laughing going up the stairs, Marc and Nick was tripping out. They both were high as hell too. The room was upstairs on the second floor, the third room on the right.

When Marc got to his room door he notice a nigga in all black fumbling with the door next to his with a hood over his head.

"You know what time it is fool".

Marc look behind him to see another nigga behind them in all black with a gun pointed at Nick. Marc turn back forward to see the nigga on the side of him had a gun pointed at him also.

"Don't do anything, stupid young nigga".

The one that had the gun on Marc put his back against the rail, and kept the gun on Marc.

Open the door fool, before I kill one of y'all niggas out here.

Nick pump faked like he had the key, not Marc. He turned around fast as he could and hit the nigga behind him straight in the mouth. It happen so fast Marc saw buddy knees buckle. The one who had the gun on Marc aimed for nick and started cutting lose.

BOOM, BOOM, BOOM, BOOM, Marc was waiting for him to slip up. Soon as he started shooting, Marc kicked him right in the chest. Flipping buddy over the rail. Nick had control of the gun him and the other nigga was tussling over. Marc pulled out that shot gun and cocked BOOM, he dam near blew buddy's whole head off. Blood was everywhere. Good thing Nick seen it coming. They ran down the stairs fast as they could toward the car. The one that flipped over the rail fell in between the cars. They ran past buddy at first, then Nick stopped and turned around and walked back towards him, kicking him in the face.

"Come on bra we got to go." (Nick wasn't trying to hear that shit.)

"Bitch ass nigga, you shot me too".

Buddy was still trying to crawl, Nick stood over him pulling out his 38. Special BOOM, BOOM, BOOM, BOOM, BOOM, trying to off that nigga. Nick tried to drive but he couldn't, that lil shot in the arm had him acting like he was about to die or something.

Chapter 41 One man Dead

Come to find out the nigga who Marc kicked over the rail was Jay, Slim's brother. Nick hit Jay 5 times and he still lived. The hotel shooting was all over the news, one man left dead and another one in ICU fighting for his life. It had gotten back to Queen that Marc had something to do with the shooting.

"Ja'Marcus what the fuck is wrong with you boy?"

"What you talking about now ma?"

"Nala told Joel you and Nick killed somebody. Marc you are really stressing me the fuck out right now".

Don't let them folks hype you up ma, I ain't did nun.

"I'm im Colorado right now I got something to tell you, when I get back. No more secrets. I love you son be safe".

Nick stayed off the seen for a lil while till his arm heal. They charged Jay with Armed Robbery and Murder, the body was on his own home boy. It wasn't know telling what he told them folks. Shit started getting hot on their end. The Sheriff Department was show all three of their pictures, asking questing about drugs. SWAT kicked Kia's door in and found 6 pounds of mid. Marc paid Nick's baby brother Kwame 5,000$ to take the charge cause the weed was his. Jose was telling Marc to leave town. Marc was making about 15 racks a day on a slow day. 20, 30 thousand dollar days came often. It wasn't know leaving.

Joel was trying his best to get Marc to move back to Georgia. But Columbus wasn't his home Detroit was. It was a lot of money in Columbus but it was small. If half of the nigga from Columbus that was getting money moved else were, they could take off. That shit was just too small.

Christmas night Marc post bond for Kwame to get out of jail. The city was live as a fool. Marc was in the Cut Dog on the 30 tonight. All yellow with the white top and white rims. 442 under the hood, that bitch was snatching.

Club Snake was the most turned up teen club in the city. DJ and was in the car with Nick in his T-top Thunder Bird on 26's. Most of the young niggas out there didn't even have cars, these niggas was mounted up like grown folks.

It was 40$ to cut the line and walk straight in the club. It was worth it doe, that bitch was long. The club was thick as hell. Nala and her crew was on the dance floor. Rich Homie Quan had the streets fucked up at the time. This was one of them club that would sell the kids liquor and everything. Bout three cups of Remy Marc was on the bullshit. The whole West Side was in the building. So if it went down it was gone go down big.

Standing in the corner high as a mufucker, DJ notice a group of niggas approach them. Marc got right when he realize buddy was talking to him.

"Say dog you lil Airplane or Marc. They say that's all the same nigga".

"It must be a problem or something Rarri".

"That's why I'm trying to holla at you like a man before it be one".

"Before it be one, you tripping my nigga".

Shante, that's my baby momma dog. You need to let the lil bit go there.

(laughing)" *Man I don't fuck with that hoe like that, you tripping. I fuck with bad bitches, that hoe ain't even my type. Next time check yo hoe nigga don't try and check me Rarri. Fuck you talking about".*

Marc read the body language on buddy that he was about to try and take off on him. The shit was so slow Marc side stepped the pouch and bowed lil buddy in the back of the head. Marc was smooth with that shit. He grabbed buddy by the front of the head and pulled it down fast as he could kneeing him in the face. Marc felt he his noise broke, when he did it.

One of his home boys was about to still on Marc, Nick yocked him up ASAP. Holding him from behind up off his feet Nick slammed him face first. He couldn't even protect his face if he wanted to. {BOOM} that nigga was out cold. Flopping on the ground like a fish out of water. A big brawl broke out in the club. BOOM, BOOM, still trying to fight Marc didn't know were the shoots was coming from. That's when Marc realize it was about three or four niggas in the club shooting. Everybody was trying to get out the club. When Marc and DJ got outside the club they started shooting again. BOOM, BOOM, BOOM, BOOM, BOOM, BOOM, It seem like one of the niggas was shooting at Marc. Marc jumped in the Cut Dog and fishtailed out the parking. As he was flying out the police was turning in. It was about 6 police cars, when Marc almost lost it and hit the car coming out the parking lot the last car came behind him.

The Cutlass was running out the ass. Marc was doing about 110 mph, with 4 cars behind him. All you could see was the lights on his digital dashboard as he played through traffic.

After blowing the red light Marc tried to make the left on Rice ST and lost control of the car. For some reason Marc could feel his right feet. His whole leg was burning. Marc ran head on into a tree. He black straight out. It took Marc a second to try and shack back. When he got the car door open, he rolled out the car. Trying to stand up he realize he was shot. By then the police was everywhere.

DON'T FUCKING MOVE!!!!!!

It was every bit of 100 police out there. Marc was fucked up he was already wanted for shooting Slim.

Chapter 42 Marc and Nala

Marc woke up in the hospital, hand cuff to the bed. The Dr. had his right leg levitated from the gunshot wound to the thigh. The wreck split Marc's eye and made him bite a hole thought his own lip as well. Nala and Kia sit up at the hospital with Marc the whole time. Queen was still on her way back from Denver. For some reason Queen was back and forth to Colorado a lot lately. For about the last three months, she had been going up there spending weeks with family Marc didn't even know she had. Queen was gone so much she didn't even know Marc was hiding his money in the house. Marc and Nala was starting to fuss too much he didn't feel he could trust her like that anymore.

Nala was in and out the hospital room, DJ stayed by Marc's side the whole time. By time Queen made it back home the police had already took Marc to the RYDC. Wasn't know getting him out of this one. Marc had been on the run for 17 months, the judge had a hold on him for a bench warrant for skipping court. On top of that the chase and wreck left him with 20 more charges and a totaled out cutlass.

The JCO put Marc in see pod. This dorm was for older and violent juveniles. Walking to the cell the officer assign Marc he locked eyes with a nigga doing push up's. Marc knew he knew body from somewhere but wasn't sure were, he just kept on walking to his cell. Jamar walked in the room behind Marc. Jamar was from the hood to, he had been riding for about a year now for robbing a liquor store on the South Side.

"What's up Lil Airplane, I been hearing good things about you out there bra".

"What's up Rarri? I just been cooling. You know me".

"My nigga. I want to sit down and kick the shit with you about the hood, but I got to keep my eye on this lame ass nigga Jay".

"Oh that fuck nigga in here bra".

"Yeah, he been in here popping to, about what he was gone do to you and Nick when he caught one of y'all".

"Fuck that nigga, he can get a one if he want one. I done bar no nigga. I know he can't whoop me".

In the dorm animosity was in the air. You could look around the dorm and feel the vibe something was about to go down. Jay was in the back of the dorm bouncing around like a boxer trying to hype his self up, the bathroom was the only blind spot dorm that the camera couldn't see. Marc let Jay put on for a second talking shit then went back there Jamar snapped on the whole dorm. *"Y'all fuck niggas better not crowed it either. Or we gone be in here fighting."* Jamar was so big and ripped up, nobody in there wanted any part of him.

Marc slipped super bad off the rip, when he tried to take his shirt off. When the shirt was over Marc's head Jay stole on Marc knocking him to the ground. Hands tangled all he could do was ball up, even know Jay hit like a bitch.

Bitch ass nigga, y'all niggas tried to kill me.

Jay got off a few likes, Marc was in a fucked up position he couldn't get right.

"Nigga let my home boy get right nigga. Get up Rarri".

"Yeah get up fuck nigga".

Jamar had push Jay off of Marc letting him get up off the ground. Marc hopped up ASAP, tossing the shirt to the ground. Jay had Marc's mouth bleeding from where he bit his lip. Jay threw a left Marc side stepped him, but his vision way blurry so he couldn't see that good to land a perfect pouch. Jay just started swinging crazy with no rhythm. Marc took one to land a mean upper cut. Grabbing Jay by the collar of his shirt catching him with bow after bow. After about 5 or 6 bows, Marc pushed Jay up off him and swept his feet from under him. Before Marc could get over Jay good "YOU GOT IT FOLK" Marc could see the fear in his eyes. Marc kicked Jay in the face, then just walked back to his cell to get the blood off of him. Jamar was sitting behind Marc while he was cleaning himself off.

You good bra, I didn't know you had them hands like that.

I'm good my lip hurting like a mufucker doe. You know me and Nick use to be in them kick boxing classes.

I remember back in the days Nick use to be in all that shit. You got to teach me how to use them bows like that Rarri.

Fasho, I know I'm stuck in this bitch for a lil while.

Marc had fucked Jay up bad. Knocking one of his teeth out at the bottom, and putting all kind of knots on his head. Marc knew if he wasn't limping he would of sho nuff beat his ass. That set the stander of all them nigga, Marc was the head Rarri around this mufucker.

Chapter 43 Keisha

See if y'all niggas go to prison, they gone kill y'all ass playing with this Rarri shit. Marc tell these fools were you daddy from man.

You know he from that C-Town. They say my daddy use to fuck around out here too doe. We lived up here one time when I was young but we didn't stay long, we moved back after he died.

All day in all Marc heard was Rarri this and Rarri that. King Charlie did this, OG pull did that. They knew more about Charlie then Marc did. It was two things Marc didn't respect about his father. How he killed his own Cousin and let his bitch kill his son mother and get away with it. Everybody knew Marc was Rarri but he stayed to his self, working out all day. Nala wasn't keeping it real with Marc. Queen would come and see Marc once a week unless she was out of town. Nick and DJ kept min on the phone for Marc. DJ had been telling Marc Keisha kept asking about him. Keisha was a older lil chick from the hood.

She was fine as a mufucker, she just couldn't walk any more. A nigga shot her in a drive by, trying to shout Slim her baby daddy. That weekend came up and the officer called Marc for viso. When Marc walked into the visitation room Queen and Nala was sitting out there waiting on him. Marc hugged and kissed Queen and sat down.

"What's up Ma?"

"So, you really not goning to speak to me?"

"For what? We ain't talked in 5 months. We don't need to talk now. I f my momma wasn't right here I'll tell you how I really feel about you Bitch!".

"Ja'Marcus watch your mouth".

I'll just wait in the car cause his lame ass not bout to talk to me like that.

By, what you waiting on.

Nala got up and walked off from the table.

"She called me this morning like everything was all good. I didn't know y'all wasn't talking".

"Oh, that is over with Ma".

"I found that money in your room boy".

What you doing all in there.

Yo uncle came to the house to meet OX and stayed in your room and I cleaned it back up and found it.

You counted it.

Yea, it was 119,000$. I put it up for you. You got me sending you all my dam money like you broke.

LOL I got some for you when I get out.

Marc never counted the money before. But he knew he had a lot. Knowing he had that money saved up, it made his time fly. Nala could have that truck that bitch didn't have a dime of Marc money when he went to jail. Keisha and Marc started writing each other. Marc let her know that he was looking for a relationship or nothing. Talking on the phone every day for two months straight Marc was starting to catch feeling for her. Keisha was a real down to earth type of female. She already had a son name Cat eye. He loved to talk to Marc when he called.

Visitation came, Marc was sleep when they called his name over the intercom. Queen just told Marc two days ago she was in Denver like always. Marc got up washed his face and brushed his teeth and went up there.

Queen was sitting at the table yelling over her shoulder, *"Yeah them kind right there"*.

Marc looked towards the vending machine and saw Keisha standing there buying him some snacks. Marc didn't see a wheel chair know where in sight. Keisha had her hair done in a Mohawk. A cute lil outfit with some fly lil Nikes on.

When she saw Marc walk through the door she couldn't stop smiling. Keisha was walking on her own, but she had to take small steps at a time. It was a blessing to see her waking across the floor, she came along way.

Hey son, you getting big boy.

What's up ma, what's up with you miss lady.

Nun just chilling happy to see you, what you been doing sweetheart.

You know I just be working out, trying to keep my head up so you can see my waves.

LOL boy you hell. I been telling you that's all I'm doing. Trying to get my leg right, cause I know my pull up game gone have to be strong on these hoes when you hit these streets.

Ja'Marcus this girl so crazy.

For real ma.

A look Keisha I need you to holla at yo baby daddy and see what he gone do. Is he gone take the lil money or what.

You know I don't fuck with that nigga like that but I'll pull up on him when I get to my car.

Tell him I'll give him 10 bands, fuck it.

Chapter 44 Marc

Therapy was working great for Keisha. She was walking better than ever. Keisha told Marc she love him, cause if it wasn't for him motivating her she would still be in that wheel chair. Keisha was two years older than Marc. All she did was work and fuck with Marc some kind of way. If it was coming to see him or talking to him on the phone. It took Keisha about a month to catch up with Slim broke ass. Keisha took Slim down to the lawyer office herself for him to sign the affidavit. Then gave the nigga the money.

The lawyer got Marc in court fast after they got the agg dropped. For reckless driving and all the other charges the judge gave Marc 15 months. That left him with 4 ½ more months sever. Marc walked out the gates 18 years old 6'2 187 pounds of muscle. Waves on bee hive. Queen came and picked Marc up, he didn't even tell Keisha he was getting out.

No one knew Marc was getting out. Keisha, Sonya and DJ was standing in Keisha pulled up in the yard when Queen pulled up. Keisha was the only one paying the car any attention. When Keisha notice Marc getting out the car she dropped everything in her hands and ran towards him.

Bra, my mufucking nigga home.

Keisha jumped up in Marc's arms. He kissed her as he spent her around in circles. DJ was trying to give Marc some dap, Keisha wouldn't let him she was all over him.

Gone now DJ you gone get yo time with him.

Cateye ran out the house and grabbed Keisha by the leg.

Ma I'm gone tell Marc you out here kissing that boy.

This is Marc cat.

"Know it's not Marc in jail".

"This me lil homie".

"Yes, now I get my bike and Xbox 360 now ma".

Queen took them to her house, and dropped them off she had a flight to catch. Some nigga had her fucked up, up there in Denver she thought Marc couldn't tell. Queen let Marc know where his money was at before leaving. Marc and Keisha kicked it all night. When Cateye went to sleep the fucked till the sun came back up. Nala didn't have shit on Keisha. Keisha was a lil porn start. A nigga could get use to fucking something this good every night.

Chapter 45 Nala and Keisha

Queen lived in Sky View, most black people from Sander Ville don't even see houses that look like these. Big ass lakes, ducks running around, white people walking dogs, this was a long way from where Keisha grew up at. Keisha was in a daze looking out the window from upstairs. Marc walked up behind her. You could see Marc's two cars on the grass, Queen took the BMW truck back from Nala after she did a hit and run in the truck. Marc gave Keisha a tour of the house. The cars to the right of the yard belonged to Charlie, Queen didn't even drive none of the. Marc had 6 pit bulls running around the back yard, all them was 3 years old. Cateye was terrified of the dogs. Marc let Keisha get a good look at his daddy's Ferrari 599 Queen kept under a car cover.

Queen left Marc's money and both sets of car keys down stairs in the basement inside a safe. The safe was in the floor under the pool table. The combination was Marc's birth day. Marc took 30 racks out the safe and the keys to his truck. He had to get something to put on, Marc couldn't fit none of his cloths any more. Marc put half of the money in Keisha purse.

"Marc what you bout to do with all that money?"

"Bae you know I don't got know clothes. I want to get y'all some stuff. Just come on".

"Ja'Marcus how much money is that?"

"A lot man, just come on please".

Well you need to hold my purse yo self with yo smart mouth ass.

The shit talking died fast when they got inside the mall. Everything Keisha and Cat wanted Marc bought for them. All three of them had about 6 pairs of shoes. Just to fuck her head up Marc stopped at one of the stands in the middle of the mall and bought Keisha a 1,700$ promise ring. The promise was they would have a baby. On the way home

Marc stopped at the Waffle House to get a bite to eat real quick. Nala walked inside of the restaurant with some nigga and did a double take when she saw Marc sitting at the table. She speed walked over to where he was, she didn't even see Keisha so locked in on him.

"Oh, so you wasn't goning to tell me you was out?"

"For what? I don't fuck with you".

Nala we cool and all but he with me right now, y'all need to caught up on y'all own time.

Oh what's up Plane when you got out.

When Nala's lil friend spoke to Marc it seem like she got mader, storming off. The waitress came with Marc's order and they left. Keisha had attitude the whole ride.

Ja'Marcus please take me home.

For what, why you tripping for.

I'm not with this shit folk, if you want to fuck with that hoe go head. I'm not bout to even start playing these games with you for real man.

What games I ain't even did shit, you tripping man. Come on Cat help me get these bags.

Cat don't get yo ass out this car, I want to go home Marc.

Marc got Cat out the car and took him in the house along with the bags. He opened her car door and carried Keisha in the house.

I want to go home Ja'Marcus.

Marc laid Keisha on the sofa, taking her shoes off so he could rub her feet. Keisha was crying while she laid there.

She couldn't even look at Marc.

Ja'Marcus you just don't know how much I love you man.

Keisha I fuck with you my nigga. I know you a rider baby girl. Stay down I'm bout to show you a whole another life real talk.

Chapter 46 Good Morning!

Queen was gone out of town so Keisha got up early and cooked breakfast. Standing over the stove in nothing but some boy shorts and a tank top. This was the first time Marc got a good look at Keisha's leg. The hollow point all most took her whole dam calf muscle off. Other than the gunshot wound, she was flawless. She didn't know he was there till Marc started playing in her hair.

Hey baby good morning, you hungry.

Hell yea, I'm hungry as a hostage.

"Ok. I'll be done in a min".

"You look mighty happy this morning".

"I am bae, my love is home. I can see myself cooking for you like this all the time in our own shit".

"It's coming bae, sooner then you think".

"Ja'Marcus I ask GOD to send me a good man to help me raise my son. And treat me like a Queen. Now that that I found you I promise I'm not going to let you go".

Nick and DJ was there to pick Marc up time he was done eating his food. Without a plug they still was holding it down. Both of them had on about 10,000$ worth of jewelry. Showing them how to cook was the best thing ever happen to they ass. Riding around the city kicking shit with the fellas, Marc mind was really in outer space. Keisha say she asked GOD for a man like Marc. He was happy to have someone like her in his life. She wanted to be treated like a Queen, Marc wanted her to feel like a goddess. The Squad was wondering when Marc was gone get his hands back on some work. When Marc made the phone call OX was happy to talk to his grandson.

Old skool what the move is pop's.

Marc, what's up grandson, you alright.

"Oh, I'm good, just trying to holla at you".

"We good too, we just got a lot of shit on hold waiting on you to come home".

"Let's do it then, I got out yesterday".

"Well say no more. I'll have something your way before the week is out".

Just like that it was back on. Jamar wasn't a nigga with a lot of money, but he was smart as fuck. The type of nigga you needed in your circle. The powder game was where the money was at. Jamar made Marc realize that if he control the powder game all the hard was coming through him. Jamar was getting out next month so Marc knew he had to get on his shit. Being out for four days OX sent Marc 3 keys and 150 pounds; 50 of the pounds was loud. Marc couldn't beat the ticket on them 2,000$ a bag how can you lose.

Marc main man Blade wasn't fucking with the green know more he was buying 9 OZ of soft. Marc knew what he could do with the weed doe, after Marc sold Blade the work he fronted him 10 pounds of mid on top of the dope. Shit picked up fast on Marc's end. He was back like he never left. Nick saw N3 at the gas station and gave him Marc's number.

"L'l Airplane".

"Who dis?"

This N3, Fat Boy fool.

Oh, what's going on big homie.

Nick told me you was home, and you was power up with that shit already.

"I got a lil' sum going on".

"What the ticket is man?"

"Like 950$".

"That's a good number, these niggas out here talking about 1,200$ all the way out".

"Dam boy, that's high. A nigga can't make shit like that".

"Bring me a split over here you know the money good, and I need yo good cooking ass to put it together for me. I don't know why DJ thank he so fire. That lil' nigga don't got shit on you".

"Fasho, I'm on the way. You got some pots, cause I don't big homie".

"I got everything".

N3 wanted a half a brick that was a quick 17 bands, dam near another 2 bands to cook it up. Before Marc went to jail N3 was one of the only niggas in the city who use to keep that gas. Marc took a bag of the OG Kush with him to let his big homie check it out. Standing over the stove with 80 grams melted down, Marc heard someone walk through the front door. Glancing over his shoulder Marc had to do a double take. It was the same nigga he was fighting the night he went to jail. Marc had his glock 40 on him so it wasn't know pressure.

"This my son right here Marc, he bout yo age. You don't know Marc, Montae".

"I done seen him around, but I don't know him".

"I told Marc I don't sell that gas no more. I let you fuck with it. Lil homie got some good gas 250$ a zip".

"Let me check it out my dog".

Marc put the bullshit to the side and got that lil money. Montae got 10 zips of Kush for Marc. It took Marc about 2 hours too cook all the dope up. N3 told Marc he was gone put the word out he had some A1 clean. And cap off of anybody looking for some. Montae was a fool with that weed. Marc was selling him the mid for 850$ a bag. He was good to jump 2 maybe 3 pounds a mid every day. Charlie told Marc when he was young "sometimes you got to overlook the lil shit, to accomplish something big."

Chapter 47 Shit Comes With The Game

The hood wasn't feeling Marc was getting money with Montae and them blood niggas.   Marc felt why not they was getting money. On the other had Jamar had got out and he was fucking with the movement. Jamar was campaigning so hard in less than a month he had everybody in the city buying weed for him. 600$ a pound, 2,800$ a pound of loud Jamar was going stupid. The next package OX sent was 10 keys, 300 pounds of mid and 100 pounds of loud. Soon as he got his hands on the work, him and Keisha went and put down on a house they found in Caver Homes for 250,000$. Marc put 60 racks down on the house. Wasn't know way in the hell Marc could have all that shit in mom dukes house. Keisha knew Marc had a lot going on because he didn't hide anything from her. She was the type of female, long as her man came home every night she was good. She loved to see him get that money like that.

Marc kept his Kel Tec 9mm with him at all times. A small lil baby chopper that shot 9 bullets. Shit was flowing good fucking with the blood niggas for Marc. Montae turn Marc onto the nigga Kenny who was post to be over the whole lil set. Young nigga bout 22 with some heavy stain. Kenny had a lil check bout his self, Marc and Jamar pulled up on Bell ST Kenny wanted to buy 6 pounds and 4 zips of soft. Normal Bell ST don't be this thick, today it was niggas everywhere posted up. Kenny was sitting on the porch with three other niggas. He act like he didn't even see Marc sitting there. Jamar rolled the window down.

"Say Rarri, this shit don't got no legs on it".

Marc could see Kenny mumbling, but couldn't make out what he was saying. His face expression let Marc know something wasn't right. Marc set back in the seat to get a good grip on his gun and fucked around and glanced in the rear view mirror. He could see a nigga duct down on the side of his car trying to open the back door but it was locked. So zoomed in on the nigga

"What nigga?"

It was all Marc heard before Jamar opened the car door and tried to get out the car. Jamar put one foot on the ground and the young nigga jumped up and started shooting- BOOM, BOOM. He shot Jamar in the chest. Jamar fell back in the car. BOOM, BOOM, BOOM, BOOM, BOOM, BOOM, BOOM, BOOM. Marc started firing out the passenger door. BOOM, BOOM, BOOM, BOOM, BOOM, BOOM -Two niggas was running up on the driver side of the car dumping. Marc grab Jamar and took off. Marc never put the car in park from the jump. Jamar was choking on his own blood, Marc was driving the Mustang as fast as he could. Marc knew he had to get his home boy to the hospital. Tears was flowing down Marc's face trying to carry Jamar inside the hospital. Blood was all over Marc as he pasted the floor. The nurse's took Jamar straight to surgery. Jamar was admitted into ICU, he was fighting for his life. Marc phone wouldn't stop ringing. He had to turn it off to get a clear head. Keisha's phone call was the only one he answer.

"You ok bae, I heard what happen to Jamar. You good".

"I slipped up bae, I should of never started fucking with them niggas".

"It's not your fault bae. That jack shit comes with the game. Come home, let me see you".

"I'll be there in a lil while".

"I love you Ja'Marcus, be safe. Remember women and children can be careless, men can't".

"I got you bae, love you to".

Marc knew Keisha was right, he couldn't do nothing stupid. The best thing to do was put the check on him. Them bands will run you down fast. For about 30,000$ Marc knew he could get all them niggas killed.

Chapter 48 That's My Daddy

It was a war going on in the hood that Marc couldn't control if he wanted to. Jamar lil brother Sam was going ham. They was shooting at him, but him and his lil niggas was shooting they ass. Nick called Marc and told him to rush to his momma's house like something was wrong. Marc pulled up in the yard jumping out the truck with his F-&-N in his hand. It was a lot of people in the yard but it didn't look like shit was going on. Nick might have had a play it was a fire ass Lexus truck in the drive way. Kia was all over some old nigga when Marc came in the house. Nala lil sexy ass was even in there.

Ma what you got going on up in here. {Marc}

"Get out my business Marc". {Kia}

"What's up lil Airplane, dam you look like Charlie". {Yay}

"That's my daddy Marc". {Nick}

"Oh shit what's up unk, when you touch down". {Marc}

"The other day". {Yay}

"Dam unk, how long you just did". {Marc}

"11 of them nephew". {Yay}

Yay was OG status like Fatty in the Rarri Gang. Yay was one of the few niggas to get away, in the Kobe escape back in the day. Yay was telling Marc and Nick he wasn't gone fuck around in the street like that anymore, he was going out there to Denver with Queen. As they stood in the front yard talking a blue Van passed by the house. When the Van made it down the street, you could hear eight different guns going off. BOOM, BOOM, BOOM, BOOM, BOOM, BOOM, BOOM, BOOM, BOOM, BOOM, BOOM, from where Marc was standing he could see the fire jumping out the barrel of the pistols. It was niggas shooting out the Van, and niggas gunning at that mufucker. Marc knew Sam was sitting down there where they was shooting at. Jogging down the street with DJ behind him, Marc ran across a lil girl laying shot in the grass. The lil girl was Mya, Sonya's daughter. She was only 11 years old. Marc was going to wait till Jamar got out the hospital to get them niggas but it was on now.

"*Listen lil' nigga stop shooting at these niggas, just kkill one of them asses. I'm going to give you ten bands every time you knock one of them fuck niggas off*". {Marc}

"*Watch the news then nigga*". {Sam}

Montae knew it was a matter of time before a nigga pulled up on him and closed his casket. He did what was best, and told Marc everything after the lil girl got killed. Kenny was staying on Owen St. with his grandmother. It didn't take long for them to find the house, GPS was a mufucker. Vic, Marc and DJ went to the front door, Nick and Sam went to the back. In all gray Dickie suites with black mask over their faces, Vic knocked on the door with his finger over the peep hole. Kenny didn't even try to look he just opened the door. "I got it GMA" When Kenny realize what was going on, Vic had a 12 gage shot gun so close to his face he could smell the gun powder. Only safe thing for Kenny to do was put his hands in the air and walk backwards toward the living room. "Go get the back door Rarri" DJ went to the back door and let Sam them end the house. Sam went in the den and found the grandmother in the den looking at T.V. she didn't even know they was in the house.

Sam brought her into the living room. She was so cared she was talking in tongues. Kenny's baby momma Tasha was laying on the sofa with their new born baby.

"*All you had to do was chill Rarri*".

"*On big B's, I didn't have nothing to do with that lil' girl getting killed dog*".

"*Who it's gonna be you or them Rarri?*"

"*That don't got nothing to do with shit dog. Let me just hug my son dog*".

"*Do yo thang Rarri. It ain't gon' stop nothing*".

Kenny picked his son up while his baby momma hugged on him crying. Tears started flowing down Kenny's face. The grandmother joined the group hug. BOOM, BOOM, BOOM, Marc blasted the whole love triangle with buck shots. Marc was close as hell to them when he fire the first shot. They all felt the house and went to Marc's house. Marc gave Keisha the key to Queen's house and told her to take Cateye over there with her. DJ was panicking, Nike was to on the low.

"Man Marc man, you don' fucked around and shot all them folks".

Would you have felt better if we did a drive by and shot them through the window or something nigga?"

"Man, you didn't have to shoot the baby".

"Fuck that baby, go with all that pussy ass shit. Nick you over there all scared too, on that hoe ass shit".

"You got me fucked up nigga, fuck them folks".

"Vic was Sam home boy. Those lil' niggas was about that life, that's why Marc fucked with them. The next nigga they had to get was that fuck nigga who shot Jamar".

Chapter 49 Jamar

Jamar stayed hospitalize for five months. Buddy hit Jamar in the chess point blank range in the chess with a 45, the impact of the bullet made his lungs collapse. Jamar had lost a lot of weight in the hospital, but he didn't lose his pride or sense of humor. Marc gave Jamar 15 racks when he came home. Jamar would let Marc get out his eye sight when he came home. DJ pulled up with Sam in the car with him. Sam had been rocking with the Squad. Jamar loved it, he loved to see his baby brother doing good. DJ had a play for 12 pounds. Jamar rolled the window down, the tent was dark as hell on the black on black Audi A8 Marc was riding in.

"What y'all got going on thugs?" {DJ}

"Who that is lil' bra over there in the car sleep?" {Jamar}

"Hell yeah that's all that nigga do is sleep and fuss with them lil hoes, they got him so fucked up". {DJ}

"*Already know it baby boy hell*". {Marc}

"*Oh yeah! My folks told me who the shooter was with that shit with y'all too*". {DJ}

"*Run me down*". {Marc}

"*You know the lil' hoe I be fucking Shun? She said the nigga her cousin. She said she don't fuck with that nigga no way*". {DJ}

"*How she know it was him?*" {Jamar}

"*The nigga got shot that day she said. The way things happen Marc, you had to hit the nigga. She said he got hit two times*". {DJ}

Marc knew he hit that nigga, but he never heard nothing else about it. DJ gave Shun 10,000$ and she text the same night he was at her house. Timmy was sitting at the table with Shun's sister Nae-Nae playing cards. Montae was over there with Shun. Nick had a eleven hundred high booster motorcycle that he couldn't ride but Sam could. Sam was sitting on the side of the house waiting on Timmy to come out. Vic was sitting on the back of the bike like buddy on New Jack City.

Montae and Timmy came out together, they was talking so much they didn't even hear Sam crank the bike up. The motorcycle came flying from around the side of the house as they both made it off the porch. *"Check mate pussy"* was all they heard before Vic let that Mac 11 rip. BOOM, BOOM, BOOM, BOOM, BOOM, BOOM, BOOM, BOOM, BOOM, BOOM, BOOM, BOOM, BOOM, BOOM,

Marc and Yay was riding around the city chopping it up about life. Yay was going on and on about Charlie like he was trying to tell Marc something. They was interrupted when N3 called Marc tripping.

"Which one of y'all punk son of a bitches shot my fucking son".

"Bitch ass nigga, we didn't have nothing to do with that shit".

"Y'all fucking with the right one this time. You fucking with a real OG nigga".

"Fuck all that bullshit you talking about. You better be lucky they didn't kill his pussy ass to fool".

Marc hung the phone up on N3. Yay asked Marc why was he fussing with the nigga anyway.

"Nephew, I'm trying to holla at you about some real shit and you arguing with this nigga".

"You know my lil home boys shot the nigga son, you know that nigga N3".

"The nigga Wayne, Kia fucking with".

"Yeah, that old ass nigga he not talking about shit for real".

N3 called back. Marc said *"hello"* and put the phone on speaker phone.

"I'm going to kill yo momma nigga and yo kids bitch ass nigga".

"Oh yeah, that shit sound good folk".

"You think I'm playing bitch?   You think I don't know nothing about you nigga?   Kia gave me the heads up on you boy when I was about to rob yo fuck ass one time".

N3 hung the phone up.

Chapter 50 In The News

Marc was trying to tie Cateye shoe when the news came on. Every time Cat put on some cloths he thought he was the freshest lil nigga in the world but couldn't tie his own shoes. The news was just going off when Marc walked in the den with Keisha.

"What they was saying bae?"

"Talking bout them two boys from the Eastside that got shot the older day. You know one of them died?".

"I heard".

"Somebody else from the East Side got killed last night to. They say his name was Wayne, they called him N3".

"LOL, man that old nigga, hell boy".

"What you talking bout Ja'Marcus, please tell me you didn't have nothing to do with this shit bae".

"Chill man; you know I been here with you all night".

Getting to the hood to get the run down on last night. The whole Squad was at the spot already when Marc got there. Nick was in the back with a lil skit {freak bitch} freaking, DJ, Sam and Vic was in the living playing NBA 2K on the PS4.

"Man y'all heard what unk did?". {Marc}

"Shit, I was there Rarri". {Sam}

"Run us down baby boy". {DJ}

"This nigga unk dead ass serious Rarri. He called me last night talking bout I remind him of Kobe, let's put some work in. You know me I'm with the shit. He said we need a hot box. The lil nigga round the corner had a lil S-10 pickup truck. I gave they lil ass a dub to let me use it. I thought unk was trying to hit a lick or something. The truck had a chain attached to the back of the truck. We pulled at club STUNTA that bitch was thick. Kia had already told unk the nigga Wayne stay in there on Friday nights. Yay text the nigga Wayne for Mrs. Kia's phone. "I'm in the parking lot.

I know you got to go home to your bitch tonight. Let me suck that dick one good time before you go in baby.")   You wouldn't believe how fast that thirsty ass nigga came running out the club for that head. Mrs. Kia must be a fool on the head of that dick".

"We were parked on the side of the building when Wayne came around the corner. Wayne walked right pass the truck. Yeah, he hit Wayne in the back of the head with a two by four and he knocked him clean out.   He then toss him on the back of the truck. Unk told me to pull off. I bent two corners and pulled over to the side of the road like unk told me.   This nigga had wrapped the chain around Wayne's neck and pushed him out the truck. I got back on the passenger side of the truck and unk started driving. With no lights on unk drug that nigga bout eight blocks. Then got out of the truck and shot that nigga in the stomach. I heard that nigga say "who you gon' kill."   We left the truck right there on Garden St. then walked to the Circle K and called a cab to take us back to the hood". {Sam}

"Uncle Yay crazy as hell Rarri, all that shit about him trying me for y'all shooting Montae ass". {Marc}

"Fuck that nigga Montae, we should of killed his pussy ass too".

"That's what I told that fuck nigga the other day". {Marc}

Yay would come to town bout every two, three months to fuck with his kids and Kia. All Charlie old skool home boys was starting to get out of prison. Yayo was back in Fla. Getting it in. Marc remember Yayo he didn't really know Yay like that just had heard of him a lot, that he was one of them loyal ass niggas. Yayo had been out about six months when he hit Marc up and told him to come fuck with him. Shit was rolling so hard for Marc it took him three weeks to get down there.

Chapter 51 Rarri Reppen Columbus

The Miami Heat was playing Detroit Pistons, Marc and Yayo had been waiting on this game to come up. Yaya didn't even know Marc was in town, they just came. Rented a beach house on South Beach, DJ and Vic was locked in. These had to be some of the baddest bitches, these niggas had ever seen. Marc already knew what Yayo wanted him to come down here for. He wanted Marc to plug him in with Jose, but he couldn't. Jose had Marc going through OX, and OX don't want to fuck with nobody. Ox didn't even want to meet Fatty. Everybody had to go through Marc.

Yayo told Marc he was at his lil bar in Overtown. Coming through Overtown, the Squad had never seen know shit like this. Them niggas was gang banging for real. They was reppen Rarri in Columbus hard but nothing like in Overtown. Niggas from up North are way different from niggas down South. Everybody in Fla had gold in their mouth, even the females. DJ and Vic's dreads look like some pretty boy shit compared to these fools. None of them niggas look like they ever been to a beauty shop and got there shit twisted.

The sports bar was pack like a lil night club or something. It was eight pool tables in the bar. They knew Marc was somebody when he walked in the door. Marc was Iced out. Big boy custom made chain of Airplane that had Rarri Gang up under it. Yayo was in a room duct off in the back of the bar. The door man was trying to pat Marc them down but Yaya stopped him.

"That's nephew bulldog, he good that's Plane son".

"Oh, lil Charlie Wollie, what's up youngster".

Marc gave old skool some dap. Yay and Yayo was in the back playing pool. Nick didn't expect to see his dad in there. Marc and Yayo set off to the side so they could chop it up.

"Nephew I know you fucking with yo granddad and shit. What you gone tax me for a couple of them bricks. I can't keep playing 30 for these bitches. You know I can give you a good ticket on it. I can do like 24".

That's what I'm talking about, these pussy ass niggas like to have they foot in my neck. But I'm bout to show these fool what to do with that money when you get it.

But what's the move for da night unk. We going to the game or what.

"I told yo folks, I am for LeBron dub tonight".

"Oh Yeah, that nigga like them Hawks".

"Nah, I'm talking bout Charlie, he like Detroit too. They got a lil' after party we can hit tonight nephew".

"Charlie's pops like the Pistons too unk".

"Still do, I just was hollering at that nigga the other day. How you thank I know where you getting the work from?"

"You talking about my daddy unk?"

"Man, don't tell me you don't know what's going on nephew?"

"I'm lost like a mufucker".

"I don't know what kind of family problem y'all got going on, but y'all need to work that shit out. Plane told me how you been handling Queen too. Shawty always been there for you sense day one.

I understand she did some fucked up shit, but she love you. Sit down and holler at her about it. I'm sure she will give you the run down now that you are older nephew".

None of that shit was adding up to Marc. His daddy wasn't dead, didn't none of it even make sense. Why would everybody know but him. Marc knew if he asked his uncle Cook he would tell him the truth. If anybody knew he knew. Marc stopped in Columbus on the way from Fla. They were going to get on a plane in Atlanta after leaving Columbus. Cook and his wife Danielle lived in Forrest Park on the far East Side of Columbus. Marc didn't tell anyone in the Squad what was going on. They all stayed in the truck while Marc went in the house.

"Hey Ja'Marcus. What you doing here, boy?"

"What's up TT? How you doing?"

"I'm good honey, you so handsome, looking just like yo daddy".

"Thanks TT. Is unk here? I just want to see y'all before I go back home".

"He back there in the back looking at T.V".

Cook had a lil room set up in the house, he called it his man cave. Cook was looking at the movie Loud Pack when Marc came in the room.

"Marc what's up nephew? I didn't know you came down here. I hear you doing yo thang".

"Who told you unk?"

"I heard it through the great vine that's all".

"Unk, I need you to keep it real with me".

"What's up? You know I love you".

"For the past 11 years I thougt my dad was dead. I went to the funeral and all; but now the shit is not adding up. I can live with him being alive, but what I can't deal with is the fact that everybody knows but me. Why not tell me unk? I'm his only child".

"You right son you got to ask him those questions. I can only tell you that he was dead for a long time but I saved him. It took everything I had to. But I'll do it again for him".

"*Talk to me unk, this some shit I feel I really need to know*".

"*A friend of Cook's told him hours before the move they was about to transport Charlie to Guantanamo Bay. Knowing Charlie, Cook knew it was gone be a matter of time before Charlie called him talking about breaking out. So he follow the helicopter in Charlie's jet to find out the exact coordinates to the prison. Cook said time they got in Cuba the helicopter lost control. The helicopter was spinning like crazy, Cook set the jet down before he got spotted. Putting the jet on the ground Cook said he started seeing bodies float out the helicopter. Then the helicopter crashed into the water. Cook got out the Plane to he couldn't believe Charlie was gone like that. Looking straight ahead of him he could see a body about 30 yards up front. Cooked jogged up there hoping it was Charlie, it was a MP doe. Cook said he could see some legs a few steps ahead. It was Charlie, fucked up bad. Head busted open, his pelvis and hip bone was hanging out his side. You could see his knee coming out his leg as well.*

The blessing of it all was Charlie still had a pose. Cook knew he couldn't leave him right there like that. He had to try and get him out of there. He used every muscle in his body to get him on that plane to safety".

Charlie had already given Cook a key to his house in Denver not to many mufuckers knew about, not even Queen. Charlie told Cook a long time ago if anything ever happen to him give Queen the money and he could keep the house. It took Cook almost years to find the money. Paying for it out his pocket Cook found the best underground Dr. there was to work on Charlie. 300,000$ was small money in the medical field. Cook almost went bank rupt, trying to save Charlie.

"Nephew do you know what kind of secret that was to keep from everybody. Yo momma, my wify, you, that shit use to eat me up at night. Then I learn how to live with it. The devil was still alive.

All cook did was read books when he was in Colorado. Charlie had a big ass book shelf, with all kind of hood books on it. Cook knew it wasn't know way Charlie had read all these dam books. Trying to find something to read Cook saw a hard back copy of the book {TRU2DAGAME}. Trying to pull the book out cook heard a latch open, the book felt stuck. The book shelf sled forward first, then to the side opening up. It was like looking inside a bank vault. Millions of dollars just sitting there cash money. Charlie had be in a coma for the past 20 months before Cook found the money. Soon's he got his hands on the, Cook could buy all the proper shit Charlie need to survive. And a lil extra shit with 90 Million dollars. It was a long 29 month wait but Charlie woke up. Form the jump the Dr. said Charlie would never walk again.

"I thought you knew nephew. Hell everybody else knew. The last time I talked to him he was talking about you and Queen not talking".

Marc couldn't believe what he just heard. When he got back in the truck, they all could tell something was going on. Nick was sitting in the back seat with Marc. Bagging out the driveway Nick looked at Marc.

"Look like you seen a ghost or something Rarri".

"Boy, I swear to god I thought I did, bra".

"What's up Rarri?"

"Man, my dad ain't dead bra".

"Say Squad".

"That's on the Squad my nigga".

"Is he in here ? Rarri, I want to meet that nigga, straight up".

Chapter 52 Loyalty

Marc was feeling some type of way like Rich Homie Quan. He didn't have any words for Queen period, it was fuck him so he felt like fuck him. Nigga picked his team and bitch over his son, Marc wasn't feeling that shit. That bullshit made Marc start keep his third eye open.

Kevin was from the South of the D. he was Vic's cousin. Homes seem like good folks from the outside looking in. Marc didn't use to be round the nigga like that. Nick paid cash for a brand new 100,000$ house. Nick use to talk cash shit to folks when he got up 250,000$. Marc was up dam near 800, he didn't give a dam what Nick had going on. Nick had a house warming party after he got everything together in the house. Nick had all the maggots in the city was in the building. Keisha wouldn't take her eyes off Marc. Nick had a fire ass camera system set up in his house. A whole room full of monitors. Keisha walked in room with Marc and DJ.

"Say Marc a lot of niggas been telling me the work been fucked up lately".

"Me to bra, them niggas tripping ain't they man?".

Hell n'all bra, I put a camera in the spot so I can see it from here the other day. I didn't tell know body Rarri I did it. If wasn't know body doing shit it didn't matter right.

Hell yea.

Yesterday morning I peeped the nigga Kevin go in the work room while everybody way sleep. The nigga had a re-rock machine hid in the house. I saw him take about 10 zips and swop it out with that cut shit he had bra. I recorded it if you don't believe me and want to see it for yourself.

Come on Rarri you know I believe you, but I still want to see it doe.

"Nigga got us thinking he just grinding out here".

"We got to kill this fuckin' nigga; nigga".

"Already know it Rarri".

Marc shut the spot down the next day and relocated. George St. was rolling so hard Marc couldn't go far. They got two apartments at the other end of the street. For the last couple of days they was using the old spot as a freak house.

Things couldn't be better for Marc. The work was dry, it would be a couple days before I got there. One of Jose's drivers got busted. It had been a whole month sense Marc bought that M-class Benz truck. Marc was shitting on the city, peanut butter brown Benz truck, trimmed in gray. Gold 24's with the chrome lips on them bitches. Chrome mirror tent on the windows. Riding around the city getting fucked up Kevin set in the back seat behind DJ. Nick set behind Marc.

"This shit got to be bout loyalty, or it will never work.

Y'all my day one niggas. Before any of this shit was going on I had y'all niggas.

Rarri Dynasty

DJ and Kevin thought Marc was tripping, they thought that molly had got the best of him. Until he put the cd inside the dish changer. Marc was already riding on the high way. There were no other cars on the road, 1:00 a.m.. The vehicle had a T.V. in the front, two on the head rest, one on each seat. When the movie came on you could see Kevin with the re-rock machine putting cut on the dope and compressing the work back together. "What the fuck is this Rarri" {BOOM} DJ couldn't even get his words out good before Nick shot Kevin in the head. Nick pushed Kevin out the car at the light getting off the interstate. You could see Kevin's brains all over the back window. Blood was everywhere in the pack seat. A lil of the blood got on DJ in the front seat. Marc heard Nick tell Kevin before he shot him "It's level to this shit like meek said."

Chapter 53 Still Alive

Kevin's murder was unsolved mystery. People didn't know if it was a robbery or what. Marc stayed under his mother till after the funeral, to keep the light off of him and to see what niggas in the streets was saying happen to him. Fucking with Yayo and killing Kevin was the best thing going for the Squad. Yayo was buying 15 keys on top of the 30 pack OX was putting on Marc, not including the weed that was coming in. With Kevin out the picture the work was back A1 every time you dropped it in the water. Joel was moving 10 bricks every other week, wasn't know looking back now for Marc, he had formed his own dream team.

Six months passed by without Marc communicating with Queen. He wouldn't even pick up the phone for her when she called him. Keisha went to the Dr. and found out she was 17 weeks pregnant, Marc was so happy. He stopped by Walgreens on the way home to get Keisha a card and some flowers. Queen's car was in the driveway when Marc pulled up. Keisha knew how Marc felt about Queen, that she wasn't right. Marc never told her about Charlie being alive doe.

When Marc and Cateye came through the door Queen was rubbing on Keisha's stomach sitting on the couch talking.

"Hey momma, hey grandma".

"Hey Cat daddy, grandma miss you baby".

Marc didn't stop and speak to nobody. He just went up the stairs and laid across the bed. Queen followed Marc up the steps to his bed room.

"Hello to you to Ja'Marcus".

"What's up Queen?"

"Oh I'm Queen again".

"That's what grandma Jessie named you, didn't she?"

"LOL what's the problem now Ja'Marcus. Let me guess this lil bit of money blowing your head up huh?"

"I come from money, you know who my daddy is" said Marcus sarcastically.

"See the funny part of it is, yo daddy come from B.T.W. he didn't grow up with shit. Everything he had was because of me.

You acting like a real female right now, I'm not going to call you a bitch, but I'll tell you one thing I didn't raise hoes. If there is sometthing you want to ask me here is your chance. You might not get another one"; Queen was tired of Marcus walking around with his head in the air looking down her like she wasn't shit.

"If the love so real and strong, then why is our whole relationship built up on lies. That's some shit I don't understand"; Marcus said with a gentle tone.

"Ja'Marcus you will never understand what happen between me and your mother. I ask God for forgiveness every day"; tears now welled up in Queen's eyes.

"I forgave you for that, bitch. The reason I hate you now is because you know how much I loved and idolize my dad and you didn't even tell me he was still alive. What kind of shit is that".

"I swear to God son I didn't want to keep this from you. I tried to tell you. Your father didn't want you to know. He said you was ungrateful, and he would to tell you", she said with tears rolling down her face.

'Man get the fuck out my house. When you see that nigga tell him I said {original} O'Rarri do real thangs. Hoe niggas do hoe shit", he was said with anger and hurt in his voice.

Queen couldn't stop crying. Marc had never disrespected her like this before. Keisha was standing outside of the room, she heard the whole conversation. Marc was sitting at the edge of the bed. Keisha walked in the room and stood in front of Marc rubbing his head *"it's gone be ok bae keep your head up daddy."*

RING, RING, RING....

Charlie could hear in Queen's voice how upset she was. She was crying her eyes out.

"What's up love bug when you coming home I miss yo' ass".

"Tonight, for good this time to Marcus".

'What's wrong bae. What you crying for".

"I'm so sick of being disrespected by your son. Marcus he called me all kind of bitches and hoes. All I ever did was try to be there for him. One of your punk ass friends must of told him you was alive, he blaming it on me. I kept telling you over and over to tell that boy", she said sulking.

"Baby, I'm sorry all this shit keep falling in your lap like

this. Stay at home for a couple more days . I will get him out here and talk to his fool one on one", Marcus said with a deep sexy voice.

Queen was melting inside after hearin Marcus bedroom voice. She missed him so much. Hearing his voice on the phone made her feel the world, their world, her world was perfect.

"Please do bae, talk some sense into him. Let him know that I still love him no matter what".

"I will bae", Marcus said convincingly.

Marc thought he was untouchable he was getting so much money. It been a few days sense Marc and Queen got into it. It was late Marc was trying to get home before Keisha got in the bed. Today had been a good day for him, 86 racks on a Wednesday before 10:00, wasn't know telling what Friday had in store. All the lights in the house was off

but the cars was in the yard. That wasn't like Keisha to not leave the front porch light on. Walking through the house Marc didn't see Keisha or Cat anywhere. Calling her phone with no answer Marc was starting to get worried. Turning on every light in the house Marc notice a note on the coffee table in the living room.

From the looks of things family doesn't mean shit to you so I took your's. I found it funny to hear you felt I had hoe in my blood, you know the same shit that runs through me runs through you. So if hoe niggas do hoe shit, then what does a O'Rarri nigga do when a hoe nigga kidnaps his family. I'll tell you what I'll do if it was me, I'll get sum for it. LOL Love Airplane Charlie.

Marc set their reading the letter over and over. He couldn't believe this fuck nigga had took Keisha and Cateye like that. Marc had a real Squad behind him, when he told them what was going on they didn't care who it was they was ready to ride. Cook gave Marc the address to the house in Denver. They road up there two cars deep, strapped up to the max. Vic asked Marc some real shit when they say the sign that read welcome to Colorado.

You sure this what you want to do big homie. Cause I ain't gone play with these niggas. If anything wrong with sis or nephew I'm gone kill one of them nigga. Fuck who daddy they is.

I done thought about this shit a million times already Rarri. It is what it is about my family. She pregnant to bra, her and Cat all I got my nigga straight up.

Fasho my nigga say know more, it's on then.

Queen had a big house in Detroit Charlie left her, but nothing like this mufucker here. This house way two times the size. The gate opened automatically when Marc drove up. All five of them got out the cars, Yay was standing on the porch holding automatic pump. Dirty Redd was standing there with Yay, with a 45. telling Marc and his crew to come with him.

Marc walked down a long hallway. A lot of the pictures that was in Queen's house of Marc, he notice them hanging around there as he walked through the house. Walking in to what had to be the dining room, for the first time in dam near 12 years Marc laid eyes on his father. Charlie was sitting in front of a table that took up dam near the whole room. It wasn't nothing but the original niggas sitting right here. Hot, Trick, N, Yayo, Fatty, the day one Squad. These was the same niggas helping Marc get off he's packages. Standing here like they didn't know him, with big rifles that shot 100 times or better. Charlie set at the far end of the table.

Looking down at the table, Marc saw it had all kind of shit engraved in it. A big ass airplane in the middle, words everywhere Squad Life or No Life was so big it took up the whole table. Marc had all kind of shit he wanted to say but couldn't find the words.

Nick pulled the seat out and tried to set down.

Who the fuck told you to sit down lil nigga. Get the fuck up out my home boy chair fool.

Nick stood back up looking down at the table, to see it said R.I.P. Kobe. In all the seats no one was sitting in, it read R.I.P. with their names. Pull's name was there to, Marc felt that was some real Rarri shit. Even know they was dead and gone they still had a place at the round table. In front of the chair Marc was standing in front of said "Much Luv Thug, R.I.P. MJG" Charlie got Marc's attention when he started talking.

It took all of this, if you wanted to holla at me why you just didn't say so.

My nigga, I don't give a dam about you. Were Keisha and my son at.

Y'all lil niggas thank y'all bad. In my prime, I would of killed all y'all lil pussy asses. Nigga you all in your feeling about her killing yo momma. If you was real as you say, you would of off her ass yourself. It wouldn't be no reason to be mad at me. You know why you can't do nun bout it, the same reason I couldn't. Cause without the bitch you wouldn't have shit. All that Jose and OX shit wouldn't be possible without Queen.

Marc heard the side door open, and someone walk in the house.

"Ma, when my daddy coming? I want to see my daddy".

"He coming Cat. You know how Marc is that nigga will be late to his own funeral (laughing)".

Chapter 54 Charlie And Marc

Later on that night Charlie and Marc got a chance to really sit down and talk. Seeing his father in a wheel chair was the last thing Marc expected. They looked just a like, the way people always use to say.

"Why not tell me, dad?"

"For real, I didn't like how handle Queen. You want to be a man, so I let you. She wanted to tell you in jail, but I wouldn't let her. She road with you and you can't even call her and see how she is doing? We all do shit we wish we could take back".

"What about with Pull? Would you take that back?"

"Yeah, niggas in the hood got the game fucked up, talking about it was bout money. I had so much money back then I use to lose 5 or 600,000$ at a time and find it months later".

"He was solid dad", Marcus said still not understanding what really went down with his dad and Pul.

"Hell yeah, moving too fast. That's what I'm trying to tell you Rarri slow down. I'm plugging you in with all my people so you can fall back. You don't have to win trapper of the month every month".

Charlie told Marc the gray carpet was laid out for him. Only thing he had to do was lead. Marc stayed in Denver for five days. Charlie sent Marc back with a clean ass Tommy gun with a 100 round drum on it. When Marc made it back to Detroit all kind of shit had done happen. Someone had broken into their new spot. All the flat screens was missing, 25 pounds of mid and a half a brick. They was gone kill who ever didn't it, it was just a matter of time before it came out.

Sam was severing Mrs. Reda like always on the first and notice the T.V. she had hang on the wall. Sam knew that was one of the T.V.'s out the spot. Sam asked her, where did she get the T.V. from. Without thinking she answered, *"My son Will gave it to me the other day."*

Marc got Will's house shot up that same night. Word on the street, Will had a chopper and was acting like he was looking for Marc. That was some bullshit. They were riding around looking for his ass every day.

Chapter 55 Party House On Bell Street

Rontae was Will's home boy. The streets knew they ran together on a daily basis. Sam was driving the smoke gray RC F Lexus Coupe. Them young niggas didn't know what they got into, not for real. Rontae was the first one to walk out the store on 3rd Ave when Sam road by.   Rontae couldn't see in the car from the shiny gray mirror tent on the Lexus.

That's that nigga right there Rarri.

Sam stopped on brakes in the middle of the road, to let Vic get out. Vic got out the passenger side of the car, Marc had let him hold the Tommy gun. He had been waiting to let that bitch rip. When Vic got out the car good all you heard was the shells hitting the ground BOOM,

Will was about to walk out the store when Rontae was trying to run back end. Vic shot up the whole front of the store. He shot so many got dam times Rontae couldn't get away. Lil chick in the store got hit. Vic made sure he killed Rontae. He shot over 50 times back to back to make sure he was dead.

Will knew shit had gotten real. He got Jamar's number from his cousin and sent him a long ass text. *"Look homie I didn't have nothing to do with yo house getting broke in. I bought that T.V. from my lil home boy Don P., They the ones with the weed and shit my nigga I don't got nothing."*

It made sense to Jamar too; Don P was buying a zip or 2, but now he been getting 9's and shit.

The party house on Bell St. off of Wynnton Rd. use to be pack every Sunday night. The nigga Don P was out there like always. Marc, DJ and Sam was riding with Jamar in his Black and Gray Box Chevy Caprice. When Marc saw him he got hot instantly.

"Stop here, bra".

Marc got out the back seat, where him and Don P was looking at each other face to face. Don P was standing there with a few home boys and a couple of hoes. It was a lot of people. Parking lot full of pimps. There were more more people outside then inside.

"Dam my nigga. Niggas drinking Ciroc and all kind of shit on me".

Jamar had them big ass 28's on the Chevy with one foot out the car they couldn't even see Marc reaching for his strap. Sam was sitting back there with Marc he peeped what was about to go down. Sam open his back down stepping out the car. They couldn't see the AK-47 he had.

"Man catch out with that bullshit nigga, don't nun over here belong to you cuz".

"Check this out Rarri, if y'all niggas don't give me my

money, I'm gone kill one of y'all niggas that's on Charlie".

"My nigga I don't owe you shit cuz".

"Nigga who the fuck you think you talking to like that fool. You ain't gone pay that money nigga?" BOOM, BOOM, BOOM, BOOM, BOOM, BOOM, BOOM, BOOM, BOOM, BOOM, BOOM, BOOM.

Sam went crazy on their ass, Marc didn't start shooting till after Sam did. Everybody started running when the shots was fired. They jumped back in the car and pulled off. Jamar was fucking a girl on Bell St. when they made it back to the spot Kim called Jamar hysterical.

"Pussy ass nigga y'all going to jail I swear to God on my big momma grave".

"Man what the fuck you talking about girl?"

"Y'all niggas shot my sister folk. Y'all just shot bout five mufucken people".

Is somebody died Kim.

That same night about 5:00 in the morning the U.S Marshals hit Jamar's Momma house. They took the Chevy, Jamar wasn't there doe. The next morning before noon the folks had Sam. The also had warrant for Marc, DJ, and Nick. Nick wasn't even there. Marc knew he had to get the fuck out of town ASAP. They all did.

Chapter 56 In Columbus Georgia

Jose and OX was glade to here Marc was moving back to Columbus. Marc knew he could lay low in the country and get a whole lot of money in the city. The Foxy Lady was the top strip club in Columbus for black folks. Marc didn't really do the strip clubs in Detroit because the females couldn't get necked. They say the dancer couldn't in Columbus either but you couldn't tell because these hoes didn't never have on nothing. Marc, DJ and Vic set all the way in the back. DJ order 2,000$ worth of ones, Marc told the waitress to bring him the same amount back. Vic order 4 bottles of Circo and a case of Coronas. For the females that was having a birthday party sitting next to them Vic asked them what they was dranking. And got a picture of Long Island Ice Tea. The two waitress came over with the money on the platter. All the hoes in there started coming over to acknowledgw them. The lil red blond was bad as fuck. Marc was trying to get her but she wasn't talking about nothing.

Ray Ray was one of the first people Marc seen when he got to town. His uncle Fatty was back locked up for parole violation. Ray Ray was holding shit down for him. They already sentenced Joel to 18 months in a Probations Detention Center in Dawson Ga, Terrell County. Marc up his crew up on game about these G.A. niggas from the jump. You always got to watch them. A nigga hate to see you doing ten times better than them. The streets was like wolfs out here, everybody was watching your riches.

It took Marc 15 days to settle in and when he did OX sent him a package. 25 keys and 1,000 pounds of mid. Don P had died and the police upgraded the charge on Sam to murder. Keisha stayed in Detroit till the folks hit her house looking for Marc. She didn't want to be gone then the folks track her down by Cateyes school recorder. So she stayed back for a lil while, so Marc could go down there and get shit together for them.

Shit was totally different in Columbus, the dope game was tricky. A Oz of crack was only 24 grams not 28. It had been almost 5 years sense Marc been down there he forgot shit was like this. The cost of living was ten times cheaper down South. And the females was corn bread thick, nothing but hips and ass. Jamar and Nick had turned into some big tricks, they lived in the Foxy Lady. Marc had a thang for them back page bitches.

DJ hooked Marc up with one of his lil bitch friends. They was dance partner at the Gold House, another strip club on Victory Dr. Ginger looked like a lil spice girl. One of them good girls gone wild. Let her tell it, she wasn't from Columbus she was from NYC. Ginger was down here going to school at {CSU} let her tell it. Columbus State University was a pretty nice size collage, and a good place to take up Phlebotomy.

Ray Ray had the projects fucked up, moving slow but ok for him, with Fatty locked up. Ray Ray was determine to get some money, one way or the other, he had plenty of that whip shit. Marc got a spot on 6th ave and put that drop in there; and he fucked the hood up ASAP. The whole down town was copping from him. Old niggas like 4way and Kent was buying bricks from Marc. Ray Ray didn't have a choice but to shop with Marc. He knew there was noone who could beat his ticket 950$ a zip during this drought. Ray Ray saw some money fucking with Fatty, but nothing like this, Marc them was eating 800$ a pound of mid. Their phones never stop ringing. Marc kept working. He was getting money all over the C-Town. He even fucked around in lil' county towns like Warner Robins, Thomaston, Talbotton, Harris County, a lot of people thought the work was in Woodbury but they was fucking with Marc too.

Marc was getting money and partying so much, he had forgot he was on the run. They were juggen so hard, riding to foreign lands and shit. Marc had to get a house in Geneva G.A., 30 min away to be duct off. Marc was fucking with Ginger the long way now. The Molly, money and hoes had Marc losing focus and not just him, his whole click. Charlie called Marc to check on him. The shit Charlie told Marc let him know he needed to tighten up fast. *"Get you some understanding son, I been through some shit like that before. Cause when them cracker get you they gon' make you over stand you feel me."*

Chapter 57 Ginger

Ginger was a sexy lil something, with a cinnamon complexion. She was sassy as hell, that's why Marc called her his lil spice girl. At least once a week Marc would go to the club and make it rain on her. Sometime the Squad would be with him. Together they might throw a 10,000$ on Ginger in that bitch. Ginger ran with a lot of them fake high calls Baker Village bitches. She was not from here, yet she knew everybody, but I guess Columbus was small; everybody knew everybody.

Keisha moved down to Georgia, Ginger was doing so good dancing she had her own condo in Phenix City. Keisha had just had her daughter a few weeks ago, she was missing Marc. She just didn't know Ginger had Marc fucked up on the low. Trying to live a double life, Ginger couldn't tell because she was getting all Marc's free time. Keisha could, Marc never stayed out all night before. The only time she saw him now was when asleep.

Detroit didn't do numbers like Columbus, the C-Town was a gold mine. When Fatty got out, business increased ten times more. That nigga knew everybody. Joel was trying to keep up with Marc but on the low Marc couldn't keep up with him. Fatty knew all the old skool niggas in the city that was buying that real weight. T-Pot got out the Feds him Mayo, Bull and Luke they use to call there self MOB in the 90's. That was before Charlie and the Rarri Gang's time. When them niggas got out they was moving all the dope. Columbus had way more robbers than dope boys, it seem like Marc knew all the jack boys, instead of the trap niggas. It was a dog eat dog territory. Marc stood behind the Rarri Gang, and there name held weight, but they was the most cutthroat niggas out of everybody. They was killing each other.

Keisha told Marc she cooked, so he stop by Ginger's apartment to see her before he went in. This was gone be the second night straight he didn't come home. When Marc walked in the house Ginger was standing in the bathroom doing her hair. It looked like she had just gotten out the tube from where Marc was standing. The phone was laying on the counter on the speaker phone as she talked and did her hair at the same time. Ginger didn't even know Marc was in the house.

"We gon' do it man, the timing just ain't been right. You ain't even on the shit." "I'm on for real."

"So what kind of shit you really on?"

Ginger hung up the phone real fast. *"I'ma call you right back gurl"*

"Hey baby, making you my husband. I didn't even know you was in here".

"I know you didn't bitch, you think I'm stupid don't you?"

"Child boo, boy you don't even know what you talking about".

"That was a nigga right. How bout this fuck with me when the timing right shawty".

"Whatever. I'm not bout to explain myself to you. Nigga you barely come home at night. Miss me with that rap shit".

Marc got the fuck on, his feeling was starting to get the best of him anyway. And it wasn't no way he was goning to leave Keisha and Cateye. Keisha had just had Tamber too. It was good he heard what he heard out of that bitch mouth. If she wanted to fuck with that nigga, then she could go ahead. Marc didn't answer her calls for six weeks. Marc was letting it be known who Keisha was. He now took Keisha to the club with him.

The Squad had an apartment in Willow Creek on Buena Vista Rd.. The apartment was located in the back of the building. They used it to cook up work and smash hoes from time to time. Marc fucked Ginger there his first time having sex with her. He didn't know she was following him when he pulled up in the apartments, till the pink and black Delta 88 blocked him in. Marc knew it had to be Ginger, because of the car but the last time he seen it, the car was primed down but it had the 24's on it already. Marc let her stand at the window of a second before he rolled the window down. She stood there in 6inch heels, with her hands on her hips. Ginger whole left arm was sleeved out. Standing there like that you could see the R.I.P Boom and Juil on her chess the way her shirt was cut.

"What's up Mrs. Lady? You looking good".

"So it's like that? You just not fucking with me no more Marc?"

"Man I don't have time for games you playing".

"Games nigga? You the one had a bitch the whole time. Got me playing with the hoe baby and shit. But I'm the one playing? You don't even know who I was talking to on the phone that night".

"I know you was on the phone with a nigga, I know dat".

"I was; sinse you think you know everything, I'm not gon' tell you. If you love me like you say you do, you would have asked me and not jump to conclusion".

"Are you going to tell me, folk?"

"My brother Randy down here from NYC. He want to come live with me but I told him he not on what I'm on. He don't have his priorities in line. I told him I got a man who helps me. And he not about to just lay up in my house on my bill. He need to wait untill he has a job".

"So when is the time goning to be right?"

"When he has a fucking job Ja'Marcus".

The tears that was flowing down her face and the entire scene made Marc weak. He fell for the bullshit she was talking. She was so fine Marc couldn't look pass her sexy face and figure. Marc told her to park her car and come with him upstairs. Marc had a big ass play on the way.

Black Tim from LaGrange G.A. was on the way to the C-Town to get 5 bricks, he couldn't cook, so Marc put the work together for him. 3 straight drop and 2 whip. Ginger had never seen Marc with any work before but she knew he was getting it in. Ginger sit there while Marc put the dope together. For 32 racks a brick Marc couldn't miss that play. He would of cooked 20 of them for him if the check was right. It had already been rolling for Marc sense he came out. Ginger got in the car with Marc while he went to go make the play. Marc always mate Black Tim at the Rite Aid on Macon Rd. Marc made sure he grabbed his strap and put his bulletproof vest on under his jacket before they left the spot.

Black Tim was parked in the back of the pharmacy, where you couldn't see his car from the road. Tim was in his burnt orange Buick LaCrosse. Marc pulled up in his flip flop bimmer, that changed colors over 6 times grape, green, lime, yellow, seaweed water blue, and gray on 26 inch

Asanti. Marc got out his car and got in the back seat with them, with the work.

"What's up homie?"

"Just Rarri, cooling Tim what it do?"

"You know me bra. I thought you was still in that Audi.; that fucker is nice. What you over there listening to?}"

"Them Mego's, nigga, " I rather be rich then famous"; that shit there be riding fam".

"I don't even need to check that work, I know that shit straight".

"You already know it baby boi".

Soon as Marc got out the car Ginger started being nosey. She lift up the arm rest and saw 40,000$ Marc made off a 50 pound bell jug earlier before they got together. Ginger had her ear piece in her ear with her eyes on Marc as she talked on the phone.

"You got to go on and do it now bra. This nigga got so much money on him right now and he making a big boy play as we speak. ......Yeah I'm finna get him to take me to Ma house. Come on".

He had 160 band play and it wasn't even 3:00 yet. With another 40 racks in the car Marc felt he could go chill for a while. Ginger set the phone in her lap when Marc got back in the car, so her brother Randy could hear everything. She couldn't stop smiling when Marc got back in the car.

"What the fuck you smiling so hard for?"

"Cause I'm happy to be with you. Is my smiling a problem ?"

"What the hell man. What do you want to do; get some to eat real quick? I'm trying to fuck some bae".

"Ok that's cool, I don't want nothing to eat. Just stop by my auntie house on Dawson St. real quick, I need to grab something".

Marc took a right turn coming out the Rite Aid. Passing right by Keisha. She didn't see Marc at first until Cateye pointed him out.

"Ma look there go my daddy in his new car".

"See this pussy ass nigga gon' make me kill him for real. Sit back Cateye".

Keisha was behind Marc the whole time, trying to see where he was going. Marc and Ginger was smoking a blunt, she was texting the whole ride. Marc turned off Andrews Rd. onto Clover lane. When Marc made it to the 4way stop sign, he was there first so Marc had the right away. A blue Crown Vic ran the stop sign and hit Marc's BMW 640. Marc couldn't get mad or do anything stupid he was already on the run from the man and he had full coverage insurance paid for shit like this. Buddy got out the car before Marc could. Buddy had a look on his face like he didn't have any insurance. Marc was going to let the nigga pull off, it wasn't shit wrong with his old ass car. Marc rolled the window down to ask the nigga was everything ok. The nigga started walking towards the car, when he got close to the car buddy pulled out a big chrome ass pistol. Marc couldn't do anything, but duck down when homes pointed the gun at him.

BOOM, the first shot hit Marc in the Jaw and came out the other side of his neck. BOOM, BOOM, BOOM, BOOM, the next four shots hit Marc in the chess. From the impact Marc could tell buddy was right up on him. The last words Marc heard before he blacked out was.

"Come on sis. I got the money".

"Just get the fuck on. I got to be here when the police come".

Part II

Coming Soon!

"Rarri Gang Dynasty"

Jamar always told Marc that a bulletproof vest would come in handy. Two of the four bullets went through the vest. The head shot did the most damage, knocking nine of Marc's teeth out (Four at the top and five at the bottom). The bullet went in his left cheek and came out the right side of his neck. During surgery the Dr. had to cut Marc's throat from ear to ear. A tube was placed through his mouth into his stomach. A breathing machine was keeping him alive. A detective asked the nurse did she think Marc was gone make it. " *He seem strong, I have faith.*" When the nurse said that the officer hand cuff Marc to the bed and read him, his rights. Columbus had a thing if your involved in any kind of shooting, they run your name through a world wide police data base. All the warrants in Detroit popped up. A murder charge after all this shit, it was like a nigga died twice. Marc thought as he laid in his hospital bed.

There wasn't a day that went by Marc didn't have flash backs about that shit. Why the fuck would this hoe do a nigga like this? He kept playing the scene of the accident over and over in his mind. And what he heard his woman tell her brother...."*Come on sis*"

"Get *the money, I got to be here when the police come*"

Marc heard all that shit. Mouth all wired up, this hoe Ginger had really did a number on Marc. (lsaiah 54:17) was all Queen use to read Marc as he laid there. "No weapon formed against you shall prosper".

"*Son you know what you told me one time when you was young. I said Marc, why you hit that girl, you told me cause she hit me ma, I ain't going out bad. You remember that, I do. *"

Queen leaned over into Marc's ear and whispered

"Nigga yo daddy survived a plane crash, I know you can handle this lil shit"

It was a 9 ½ month fight, but Marc came out on top. After being released from the Medical Center in Columbus, Marc was expedited back to Detroit by two sheriff for the murder charge..............RGD #2.... Coming soon.

To understand this story you must remember being real and loyal are not the same thing. Family and friends will become your worst enemy's, when you mix money and drugs. Imagine a Squad that really felt they were above the law, by any means necessary; jail was not an option. Airplane Charlie stood firmly on the words Squad Life or No Life.